AT DEAD OF NIGHT

Also by Tony Whelpton

Before the Swallow Dares
The Heat of the Kitchen
Billy's War
There's No Pride in Prejudice
A Change of Mind
High Time

This book is dedicated to

Liz Freeman

who, having heard me tell the story of something which had really happened to me, challenged me to turn it into a novel

Chapter One

'Are you listening?' said the voice.

David Sumner grunted. More a stifled yawn than an answer. The next movement was from his eyes, which he was vainly trying to open, in an attempt to ascertain who was addressing him. At length he succeeded in forcing them open, but could see no one; in fact he was unable to see anything at all, which should have been less surprising than it was, given that it was the middle of the night. He turned his head to the right, and perceived only the faintest glimmer of light filtering through the heavy bedroom curtains; he turned his head to the left, and found that all was black.

'Are you listening?' the voice asked again.

The true answer, if David had been in any way capable of judging exactly what was true and what was false at that precise moment, would almost certainly have been, 'No, I'm not!', but his brain, deadened by the darkness of the night and the depth of the sleep from which he had just been awakened, allowed him merely to hear, not to listen; and all he was able to hear was the disembodied voice of a person whom he believed to be his own daughter. But in reality he was too confused to make any answer at all; he was just vaguely aware that it was dark, that he had been in a deep sleep, that he had been awoken by the ringing of the telephone, and that his daughter was asking if he was listening.

'Are you listening?' Susan's voice again, this time betraying a degree of impatience.

'Yes,' he said, still in a state of confusion, his answer being less of a true statement, more of a reflex action in response to Susan's commanding tone; he had learned over a period of many years that it was, without exception, always prudent to listen to what a daughter said, because a failure to listen would nearly always catch a father out, whether the daughter was an infant, an adolescent, or, as in the case of Susan, an adult with children of her own. But why on earth was she calling in the middle of the night?

The digital display on the clock-radio beside his bed, adjacent to the telephone, showed that it was 2.15 in the morning. His head was pounding, as was his heart; he had gone to bed early because he was suffering from a heavy cold. The effect of the paracetamol tablets he had taken had already worn off, and the last thing he needed at this time of night was a phone conversation of any kind, no matter who might be at the other end of the line, even a well-loved daughter.

With what seemed to him a more than superhuman effort, he managed to sit up in bed; he saw the time change from 02:15 to 02:16. Once more he directed his glance towards the window on his right, and, even as he watched, the glimmer which he had previously observed suddenly evaporated: it must have come from the neighbour's security light, he thought, probably triggered by nothing more than a visiting cat or possibly a fox.

It was only then that it began to dawn on him that in his right hand he was holding the handset of his bedside telephone. He had no more than a faint recollection of hearing the phone ring while he was asleep; he therefore assumed that he must have reached out with his hand on hearing the telephone ring, and removed the handset from its cradle. But how long ago had that happened? He could not have said with any exactitude, but it seemed a long time ago. Whoever his caller was would undoubtedly have rung off by now, he thought, but he strained to raise the handset to his ear none the less. Once more he heard the insistent voice of his daughter Susan: 'Can you hear me?'

'Yes,' he replied instantly, but the sound of his own voice seemed strangely blurred to his ears, as if he were in an echo chamber.

'Are you listening?' said the voice again.

'Yes, I am listening,' he assured the caller.

'This is very important,' said his daughter again, very slowly, deliberately, even gravely, enunciating each word as if to ensure it would not be missed. 'I did not call the police. It was your family who called the police.'

'What? What are you talking about? What do you mean? I don't know what you're talking about...'

But his daughter's voice had disappeared; she had rung off.

A sudden thirst overtook him, so David mechanically took a drink of water from the glass which was always by his bed at night, then glanced in the direction of his wife Margaret, who lay beside him, still in a deep sleep. How on earth had she managed to stay asleep in spite of the ringing of the phone, his speaking, and Susan's persistent tone? No, forget the last point, he thought, she wouldn't have been able to hear what Susan said, would she, even if she had been fully awake? At last his brain was slowly beginning to clear, although it was still far from returning to its normal, alert, waking state. He tried to go over and over in his mind what had happened since he had been awakened by the phone, but, no matter how many times he confirmed to himself the details of what had occurred, he was no nearer understanding the significance of what his daughter had said. What could she possibly have meant? 'I did not call the police,' she had said. The meaning of that was clear enough, even if the necessity for saying it was totally unclear. Why might she have needed to call the police? Why should anybody have called the police? But someone clearly had done. 'It was your family that called the police': the words were still reverberating inside his head. 'Your family', she had said. 'Your family. Your family...'

So who had called the police? If what Susan said was true, the number of people potentially responsible was limited: it could in fact only be one of two people, either his son Eddie, or Eddie's brother Matthew, who were Susan's step-brothers, for Susan was David's step-daughter – although David often forgot she was not his own child, for she had been in her teens when he had married her mother, and that was over thirty years previously. Nor was it a topic that was ever referred to by any of them, for in whatever permutation one chose, the relationship between David, Margaret, Eddie, Matthew, Susan – and Susan's husband James too – was as stable as any; hence it was very curious, and, the more David thought about it, utterly mystifying, that she should have made such a distinction: 'I did not call the police. It was your family that called the police.' For anybody to suggest that there was a difference between my family and your family would have been to fly in the face of reality.

So what should he do now? Go back to sleep? Not possible. The only certainty of which he was aware was that he was too wide awake now to be able to go back to sleep. He looked again in Margaret's direction and saw that she was still in the arms of Morpheus, sleeping the sleep of the just, so there was no possibility of discussing it with her at the moment. He, on the other hand, felt restless, and was aware of a pressing need to reflect deeply on what was going on.

David slipped out of bed, felt for his slippers and then crept downstairs to the kitchen. He switched on the kitchen light and at last he began to wake up properly: at least the act of switching on the light had apparently also had the effect of switching on his brain, and he was finally able to start thinking rationally about the mysterious phone call he had received from his daughter.

'The obvious thing to do is to call her back straight away, I know that,' he said to himself. 'I wouldn't normally call anyone in the middle of the night, but she couldn't really complain about that, because it was the middle of the night when she called me, wasn't it! In any case, she can't possibly have gone back to sleep – it's only five minutes since I was talking to her, and she sounded much more awake than I did!'

So he dialled the number and waited. He heard it ring out once, twice, three times. Then he heard a voice at the other end; not the voice of his daughter however, but the weary-sounding voice of a man.

'Hello, James, it's David,' he said to his son-in-law. 'Is Susan all right?'

'Yes, she's fine. Why?'

'Because I'm totally confused by her phone call. What was all that about?'

'What phone call?'

'The one she made to us about ten minutes ago.'

'I think you must have dreamt it, David,' said James. 'Susan is fast asleep beside me. She had an early night, and she went to sleep straight away.'

'Are you sure?'

'Yes, of course I'm sure. I've only just come to bed myself, because I had some work to do, and I would certainly have known if she'd made any calls. What was the call about?'

So David related to James all that had happened; James listened, and then said: 'I should go to sleep and forget about it. It obviously wasn't Susan, or I would have known about it. I would have heard her. It must have been somebody else. It was probably a wrong number.'

'But I couldn't possibly have mistaken somebody else's voice for Susan's. It couldn't possibly have been somebody else.'

'But I can assure you that it definitely wasn't her, or I would have known.'

'Oh, all right,' replied David, unconvinced. 'I'm sorry to have disturbed you. Good night.'

David switched off the kitchen light, made his way upstairs and returned to the bedroom, where, as he was getting back into bed, he heard a muffled voice from somewhere under the bedclothes.

'Are you all right, David?'

'Yes, I'm fine.'

'Can't you sleep?'

'Oh yes, I can sleep, don't worry!'

'So why did you get up?'

'I was woken by the phone ringing, that's all.'

'I didn't hear the phone! Who was it?'

David felt unwilling to recount every detail of the last half-hour at that stage, so he took what he thought was going to be a shortcut. 'Oh, it was only James, don't worry, Margaret. Go back to sleep.'

Margaret sat up in bed. 'James? What did he want? Is there something wrong? Why did he call? Is there something wrong with one of the children?'

'I don't think so. He didn't call. I called him.'

'Why did you call him in the middle of the night?'

So David found himself once more trying to describe the phone call he had received, but by the time he had completed his narrative, his audience was no longer sufficiently awake to hear his words. He, on the contrary, was more awake than he had been at any point of the night, and he lay there pondering over what had happened, what his reactions had been, and, in particular, what else he could have done and what he should do now. His son-in-law had been adamant that the call had not come from Susan, but if it had not been Susan speaking, why had he been so convinced that it was? It is true that she was not using her normal tone of voice; rather it was clipped, terse, calmly insistent, belligerent even. But there had been occasions in the past when he had heard his daughter speaking in such a tone, if she was very upset, for instance, or angry.

But if it wasn't Susan, who was it? He was almost on the point of deciding that he would never know who it was when a thought crossed his mind: why had he not dialled 1471, to find out where the phone call had originated? It was something that he very often did as a matter of course, something which he would undoubtedly have done automatically if the call had come in the middle of the day.

He got out of bed once more and went down to the kitchen, to avoid disturbing Margaret again. He picked up the kitchen telephone. As his fingers were about to touch the key pad he hesitated; suppose the number he was about to hear did turn out to be Susan and James's, what then? He dismissed the idea at once; it was more likely that the message which awaited him would say, 'We do not have the caller's number to return the call', or 'The last call was from a network which cannot transmit numbers'. If that were the case, then that would be the end of it: he would never know.

He dialled the four digits, then heard a recorded voice read out a number: a local number, but it was not Susan and James's. So James had been right; he had been mistaken, and it was not Susan's voice he had heard. He put the phone down and thought a little more. It may not have been Susan, but it was clearly somebody, and somebody to whom the message was important, and who, it would seem, was under the impression that she had delivered the message to the right person. But she had not, had she? He decided that he would return the call the following morning; he could hardly ring at this unearthly hour. But wait a minute – why not? She had called him in the middle of the night, and if the matter was as urgent as she had made it appear, she was unlikely to have just gone to bed and forgotten about it. Yes, he would call her back now. But wait a minute – what was the number? He had only listened with a view to verifying that the call had not been from Susan's number, and, apart from noticing that it was a local land-line number, he had not taken too much notice. He picked up a pencil and a note-pad and dialled again, this time ensuring that he wrote the number down as soon as he heard it. That done, he dialled the number, and waited.

He heard the ringing tone, and found himself counting the rings: one, two, three, four, five... By the time he reached twenty-five he decided that no one was going to answer, so he replaced the receiver and started thinking once more. Feeling less than confident that he had dialled the correct number, he tried again: this time he heard the 'Number unobtainable' tone. He tried again, and again, but still with the same result, so he sat thinking again. Eventually, after some considerable time during which his mind seemed to be going round in circles, he came to the conclusion that there was nothing more he could do tonight, so he went back to bed. As he climbed into bed he glanced at the still sleeping Margaret, then closed his eyes.

The next thing he knew, it was morning; sunlight was streaming through the bedroom curtains, he could hear the voices of John Humphrys and Jim Naughtie coming from the radio, for he and his wife woke up every day to the sound of Radio Four's Today programme, and then, a few seconds later, there was

Margaret's voice informing him that she had just put a cup of tea on his bedside table.

While they were sitting up in bed having their early morning tea, David related to Margaret what had happened during the night, adding to the narration his ultimate conclusion that, since it seemed unlikely that the call had in fact been made by Susan, the call was clearly not intended for him and he had come to the decision that he should not concern himself with the matter any more.

Once Margaret had got over her amazement that she could have slept through not only the ringing of the telephone but also David's speaking to the caller and subsequently getting up and coming back to bed a quarter of an hour or so later, she dismissed in a summary manner the notion that he should wash his hands of the whole thing. 'Unless you were imagining the whole episode,' she reasoned, 'the matter was clearly of great importance to the person who made the call, and also, I assume, to the person she thought she was calling. If I had made that sort of call, and had made a mistake in dialling the number and got connected to the wrong person, I would be very unhappy at the thought that the person who took the call had decided not to bother doing anything about it at all!'

'But I did do something about it!' her husband protested.

'What?'

'I tried to call back, but that number clearly doesn't exist!'

'Why do you think that?'

'Because I found out which number the call was coming from, and tried to ring back, and every time I got the line unobtainable tone.'

'Was it a local number?'

'Yes, it was. At least I know that! Well, it wasn't actually a Cheltenham number, it was a Bishop's Cleeve number, because the area code wasn't 01242, it was 0124267.'

'Well, that at least confirms that it couldn't have been a call from Susan!'

'Why does it?'

'Because Susan doesn't live in Bishop's Cleeve, silly!'

'Oh, I know that! But anyway, I could have told you the call wasn't from Susan's number even if it had been a simple 01242 number. After all, I do know Susan's number, silly!'

Margaret ignored David's attempt to take revenge, then said, 'But I wonder why the number was unobtainable when you tried to call back.'

A thought suddenly struck David. 'Oh, wait a minute, something just occurred to me!' replied David. 'Actually I didn't get the number unobtainable tone the first time, in fact it rang for quite a long time. Then I put the phone down and tried again, and that was when I got number unobtainable. And then I tried again, and again, and it was still unavailable every time. Perhaps the line developed a fault after I called back, do you think?'

'Unless you dialled it wrongly the first time. Is there any way of checking that?'

'Yes, there is. The phone stores any number you call.'

'Permanently?'

'I doubt it. It probably just stores the last five or something like that.'

'Well, are you going to check?'

'Yes, okay.' So David pressed the Redial button and saw the last five numbers that had been called. There he saw Susan's number, followed by 1471, then by two identical numbers which confirmed that he had not dialled incorrectly. 'No, I didn't make a mistake,' he said, 'so the fault must have developed in the interval between the first time I tried to call back and the second.'

'Perhaps after she made the call she realised that she had stupidly rung the wrong number, and was so upset that she threw the phone at the wall and smashed it? After that it would ring as unobtainable, wouldn't it?'

'Yes, I suppose it might. No, wait a minute! It's more likely that, even if the phone had stopped working, you would still hear the ringing tone at your end, because the tone you hear comes from the exchange, I think, rather than from the other person's phone. But I don't think that's really what happened, because the first time I rang back I could hear it ringing out. It was only when I tried again that it was unobtainable.'

'Oh, I see. Is it still ringing unobtainable?'

'I don't know, because I haven't tried this morning. I'll try now.'

So David dialled the number once more, and once more he heard the number unobtainable tone.

'Wait a minute, David, I've just had an idea!' said Margaret.

'What's that then?'

'There are certain phones from which people can make calls, but they are not able to receive calls.'

'Which sort of phones?'

'Phones in a Government department, for instance. Someone who works at GCHQ, for instance, may be able to call out, but if you try to ring them back you can't get through. I don't know, but I suspect that if you try to ring a forbidden number, you would hear the 'number unobtainable' tone!'

'That's a good idea on the face of it, but it can't be the answer in this case!' said David.

'Why not?'

'Because if it had been a call from a GCHQ phone, I wouldn't have been able to find out that it was from a Bishop's Cleeve number! Nice try though!'

'Oh, I see. So do you think that what really happened was that the line developed a sudden fault after you tried to ring back?' asked Margaret.

'It might.'

'Granted, in the sense that any fault has to have a beginning, and that could happen at any time. But equally, it might not. There's something else that's bugging me though. The caller said that it was your family that had called the police, yes?'

'Yes.'

'So the police had been involved, therefore it must have been a pretty serious matter, don't you think?'

'Yes, I suppose so, but what do you think I should do, call the police myself?'

'Yes. I think that's the least you should do. If it were me, I would also double check the number the call came from.'

'I have double checked!'

'Then triple check!'

'I did, just now! And what if it's a number that doesn't exist?'

'It can't be!'

'Why not?'

'Because if the call you got was from a number that hadn't been allocated, you wouldn't have got the call at all! You can't make a telephone call from a non-existent number!'

'Oh, of course you can't! I hadn't thought of that! So I need to call the exchange too. Good thinking! It's a good job it's Saturday and we haven't got to go out anywhere! Which do you think I should try first?'

'Don't think it matters really... No, wait, perhaps you should ring the exchange first, because if there is anything fishy, the police would need to be in possession of as much information as there is available.'

'Yes, I suppose that makes sense. I'll do it straight after breakfast.'

So, once he had shaved, showered and dressed, and had his two customary slices of toast with marmalade, accompanied by a cup of coffee, David first tried calling the number from which the call originated to check that it was still ringing unobtainable – which it was – then called the telephone exchange.

'How may I help you?' asked the operator.

'I'm having difficulty calling a certain number. I wonder if you could check it out for me.'

'Yes, sir, of course. What's the number?'

David read out the number concerned from the slip of paper on which he had written it down during the night, then waited a few seconds.

'I'm sorry,' the operator said, 'I'm afraid there seems to be a fault on that line.'

'Is there somebody working on repairing it?'

'I'm afraid I have no information on that matter, sir.'

'Would you mind telling me whose number it is?'

'I'm sorry, sir, but I'm afraid I'm not allowed to give out information of that kind.'

'Is there any way you can get in touch with the subscriber who has that number?'

'I'm afraid not, sir, until the line is repaired. Could you tell me why you think I should?'

'Well, it's quite a long story, but it might be important, because the police are involved. I was awoken by a call from that number at a quarter past two this morning...'

'If you want to complain about a nuisance call, sir, you should call the police.'

'I'm going to call the police as soon as I finish this call to you. This is what happened...'

So David finished up telling the operator the whole story, after which she was still unable to be of any material help, so he made himself another cup of coffee and sat down to have another little think.

After he had finished his coffee he finally called the police. This time he decided that a different approach was needed.

'Hello,' he said, once a policeman had answered the phone. 'I was woken by a telephone call at a quarter past two this morning.'

'I'm sorry, sir,' said the policeman, but complaints about nuisance calls should be made to your service provider, not to the police.'

On hearing the policeman's response David felt extremely annoyed, because his service provider had just told him to phone the police if he wanted to complain, and now the police appeared to be saying the opposite. He was also angry because both operator and policeman had automatically assumed that complaining was the reason for his call, even though he had not said as much. Complaint was far from being the reason for his call anyway, so David strove to keep calm, and went on to explain to the policeman that he wished to help the police, not to complain.

'Right, sir,' said the policeman, 'so how can we help you... um... I mean, how can you help us?'

David explained in detail what had happened, but the policeman still failed to understand that it had anything to do with the police. 'So what do you want the police to do about it, sir?'

David drew a deep breath. 'It's not a question of what I want the police to do, it's already a police matter.'

'Oh, I see. Can you tell me the crime reference number?'

'I'm sorry, I don't have one.'

'If you've already reported a crime, you must have a crime reference number...'

'I didn't say I had reported a crime...'

'So you mean you want to report one now... Tell me what happened.'

'But I've already told you...'

'I'm sorry, sir, but I don't think you told me about a crime...'

David sighed, then started to repeat his story of the night time telephone call, but the policeman interrupted him.

'You've already told me that, sir, but I don't see why it has to be a police matter.'

'Because my daughter – or the person I thought was my daughter – said that she had not called the police, it was my family that called the police.'

'So tell me the name of the person who got in touch with the police.'

'I don't know who it was.'

'But it was a member of your family, your daughter said so...'

'No, it wasn't my daughter at all. I thought that it was my daughter calling, but I was mistaken. Whoever it was that called me said that somebody had called the police, and I just thought that since the police already knew about it – whatever it was – it would be helpful to the police if I told them about this phone call.'

'I'm sorry, sir, but if you can't give me the crime reference number, or the name of the person who reported the crime, I can't help you.'

'But...' David tried to protest, but the policeman cut him short.

'We're very busy, sir, and I have to tell you that it's a serious offence to waste police time. Thank you for your call.'

David attempted to protest again, but it was too late; the policeman had already terminated the call.

Incandescent with rage, David came close to throwing the telephone against the wall, but thought better of it. After sitting quietly for a while he had regained at least a small portion of his composure, and even went as far as thinking that, if he had thrown the phone against the wall, he would at least find out what ring tone he would hear if he tried the number on his mobile!

Then David related the course of his conversation with the policeman to Margaret. 'That's ridiculous!' she scoffed. 'And there was I thinking the days of Police Constable Plod were all in the past...'

'Not likely!' David said. 'If that conversation is anything to go by, the brain no longer has any place in police work. It's absolutely pathetic! And all I was doing was trying to do the right thing! What should I do now?'

'Have you spoken to Susan about it?'

'No, you know very well I haven't! I've only spoken to that idiot operator and the equally idiotic policeman! I'll have another coffee, sit down for ten minutes, and then phone Susan.'

'You've already had three coffees! Don't overdo it!'

'I've only had two!' he insisted.

A short while later David did indeed ring his daughter. When she answered he initially felt somewhat disturbed, because the sound of her voice recalled instantly the moment of that call in the very early hours of that same morning, which had the effect of making him tend to disbelieve that it had not been Susan's voice that he had heard. Nevertheless he carried on with the call.

'Hello, Susan.'

'Hello, Dad! James tells me you've been imagining things...'

'Imagining things? I don't think so! What do you mean?'

'He said you thought I'd called you in the middle of the night when I was asleep!'

'I don't think I imagined anything! The call was real enough. And even hearing your voice now I can understand only too well why I was convinced it was you speaking.'

'Really? Could I really have a voice double?'

'I suppose it must be possible, because I could have sworn it was you.'

'So what did I say?'

'Well, you – or someone who sounded like you – said, "Are you listening? This is very important. I did not call the police. It was your family who called the police." You see, I recall the exact words.'

'How weird! And what a strange thing to say! All I can say is that I didn't call you, and I certainly wouldn't have said to you that it was your family that called the police. Why would I say that? You are my family! Why would I suggest that you have a family other than the one I'm a member of? And more to the point, how could you even have thought that I might say something like that?'

'Because I know your voice! After all, I should do, because I've known you for thirty-nine years!'

'Nearly forty, Dad!'

'Okay, nearly forty. But normally when you call, I hear your voice on the other end of the line and you don't need to announce yourself, I know exactly who it is from the sound of your voice.'

'Perhaps you were still half asleep... What time was it?'

'About a quarter past two.'

'There you are, you see... Anybody would be more easily deceived at that time of the night, especially if they'd just been woken up from a deep sleep.'

'Yes, I suppose that's possible. But it's uncanny that somebody else could sound so much like you...'

'Well, I should just forget all about it if I were you.'

'I wish I could! But there are too many things that concern me. I mean, someone must be in real trouble if the police are involved, and it's obviously a family problem – a family that's divided perhaps – and then there's the fact that I know the number that she was calling from, but when I try to ring her back, I can't get through. And the police aren't interested...'

'Oh, you've spoken to the police about it, have you?'

'Yes, I got some constable who was as thick as two short planks – no, correction, as thick as seven short planks, if not more! And he just didn't want to know. He even came close to charging me with wasting police time! But like it or not, I really feel involved now, and I'm worried about that girl and the person she thought she was talking to when she called me, to say nothing of that person's family who called the police...'

'Well, I'm afraid I've got to go out, Dad. Sorry to leave you in the lurch, but I can't really think of anything helpful to say!'

'All right, don't worry. I expect an answer will emerge eventually. Bye for now!'

'Bye, Dad,' said Susan.

When David had finished speaking to his daughter he resumed talking to his wife. 'You know,' he said, 'I'm really worried about that girl.'

'Susan? Why? What's the matter with her?'

'No, not Susan! I mean the girl who called last night. I'm convinced somebody is in real trouble. Either that, or else they're up to no good! Whichever it is, I feel I can't let it go...'

'Then don't! Use it!'

'What do you mean, use it?'

'Exactly what I say. Use it!'

'I'm sorry, perhaps I'm a bit dim through lack of sleep or something, but I really don't know what you mean.'

'Well, what is it you do for a living?'

'You know very well what I do for a living! I'm a writer.'

'Exactly! And usually you're a highly imaginative writer too. But it sounds as if your imagination has suddenly deserted you...'

'Oh?' David seemed surprised.

'Now just listen to me. What does a good story need to get off the ground?'

'Oh, all sorts of things! Strong characters with interesting things happening to them, conflict, drama – the list is endless!'

'Yes, that's right, but there's one thing you haven't mentioned that you're always going on about whenever you start a story...'

'I really can't think what you mean!'

'Really? Oh dear! Everything's going to pot, isn't it! Perhaps it's because it's Saturday, and as a professional writer your brain doesn't work on Saturday... Or perhaps it's because you were up half the night! Am I going to have to tell you?'

'Yes, I think you'll have to, because I have absolutely no idea what you're talking about!'

'What does a fisherman have on the end of his line?'

'A fisherman? Oh, I don't know... Bait, I suppose.'

Margaret sighed. 'No, I don't mean bait... Of course a fisherman uses bait, but what stops the bait from falling off the line?'

'The hook, I suppose...'

'Ah, we've got there at last! The hook, exactly! How many times have I heard you complaining because your hook wasn't convincing? And the first time I heard you say that, I hadn't the first idea what you were talking about! You had to explain to me in words of one syllable how every story needs to get off to a good start, and how professional writers call that a hook. Now just think about that telephone call you had in the middle of the night... Isn't that a perfect, ready-made hook?'

David at last showed signs of grasping what his wife was trying to suggest. 'Yes!' he said. 'I hadn't thought of that! Perhaps you're right...'

'Can I have that in writing?' Margaret asked. 'Because if the key to a good story is an effective hook, I'm going to claim half the royalties on this one!'

'You already get half the royalties I earn anyway, if not more! But the problem with this particular hook is that I don't know where the story's going. Or, to be more precise, I have at least half a dozen possibilities, and I don't know which one to choose!'

'Why restrict yourself to one possibility? Why not use all of them?'

'Because I'm a short story writer. It would be too long.'

'But as long as I've known you, you've always said that one day you would write a novel…'

'Oh, I know I've said that, but there's a world of difference between saying it and actually doing it!'

'Well, now's your chance! And if you don't want to do it, I'll do it for you!'

'I might hold you to that!'

'And I might very well do it too! I rather fancy giving up nursing – especially the night shifts! Just imagine me sitting around doing nothing, pretending I'm hard at work…'

'Hey! I really do work hard!'

'I know, darling, I'm only pulling your leg! But seriously, I really do think this idea might work! I can see it all falling into place before my eyes.'

'I wish I could! So what's your plan?'

'Okay, here goes… It's a story about a writer… let's call him David…'

'Yes, let's!'

'Shut up, David, or I won't tell you!'

'Sorry, darling! My lips are sealed.'

'Good! Then keep them sealed! Well, David is a writer, and he has a phone call in the middle of the night – just like you did. And he can't stop thinking about it, and dreams up all sorts of scenarios to explain what the phone call was about. How many possibilities would you say you have running around your brain at the moment?'

'At least half a dozen, but maybe more.'

'Good. Anyway, David's brilliant wife comes up with a suggestion, because he's always been a short story writer and doesn't quite know how to make the transition to being a novelist...'

'Yes, you need a stupid husband to go with a brilliant wife,' David laughed.

'Shut up, or I won't go on! Anyway, his wife's suggestion is that he makes up a short story about each of the possible scenarios that are going around his head, say, six, eight, ten stories – all self-sufficient and independent, but plausible interpretations of what the mysterious phone call might have been about...'

'Oh, I see, yes, I'm getting the idea... But I can see one snag.'

'What's that?'

'It's a very big snag too. The trouble is that for that idea to work you'd really need to know what the true version is.'

'Why? I don't think you would. I mean fiction is fiction, isn't it? You're perfectly capable of making up a story which caps all the stories that have occurred to you so far, and if you say that's what the phone call was really all about, nobody's in a position to argue with you, are they? And then there's always the possibility that you might suddenly discover what was behind the phone call...'

'And what if it turned out to be a boring, mundane story?'

'Then embroider it! The author is God!'

David laughed. 'Oh yes! If only!'

'But it's true. You're the only creator of every story you write. Now at the beginning of this story there is a real phone call, and that phone call raises all sorts of questions. But just imagine you had dreamed up that phone call. It would still be a cracking start to a story, wouldn't it? And you could make up any story you liked to explain it, don't you see?'

'Yes, I do. What a good idea! And what a brilliant wife I have!'

It was Margaret's turn to laugh. 'I told you I was brilliant! I've been trying for years to convince you of that!'

'Well, now you've convinced me! So what do I have to do to make you think I'm brilliant too?'

'Just write the stories, that's all...'

'Yes, I will do, just as soon as I get back.'

'I didn't know you were going out. Where are you off to?'

'I thought I'd just pop round to have a word with Gerald...'

'Gerald?'

'Gerald Pilgrim.'

'Why are you going to see Gerald Pilgrim?'

'Because he's a retired police inspector, and I thought it might be a good idea to tell him about the call I had, and see what he makes of it all. I might even get some useful ideas for my book!'

So David popped round to see Gerald Pilgrim, who lived next door but one. 'Hello, David!' said Gerald when he answered the door. 'What can I do for you?'

'I just wanted to consult you about something that happened last night.'

'Oh? What happened?'

'I had a phone call in the middle of the night...'

'That was thoughtless of someone! Was it urgent?'

'Maybe it was, but I don't really know what to make of it myself, and I thought that the mind of a policeman might set me on the right road...'

'A very old-fashioned policeman, mind! Don't forget I've been retired for two years!'

'Old-fashioned I can take – it's the new-fangled I have problems with!'

'I know what you mean!' Gerald laughed. 'Okay, tell me the story...'

So David related to Gerald the story of the telephone call he had received, and what action he had taken since.

'I see,' said Gerald when David had completed his narration. 'I can see why you were mystified – that sort of thing can be very disarming.'

'Too right it can! The stupidity of the policeman I spoke to on the phone didn't do my temper any good either!'

'I should go easy on the young copper, if I were you! You don't know anything about him, I assume?'

'No. He didn't even tell me his name.'

'He was probably a very inexperienced young chap, you know. It might even have been the first time since he joined the police force that he had had to answer the phone.'

'I suppose it might have been...'

'Or perhaps he'd been on duty all night and just before he was due to go home his sergeant gave him something awkward to do and then the phone rings and there's some old bloke who starts rabbiting on about something he probably dreamt...'

'I didn't dream about it!'

'Maybe you didn't, but you get all sorts of funny calls first thing in the morning in a police station!'

'All right, I'll go easy on the young copper. I suppose he can't help it if he's still wet behind the ears... But what would you make of the call I had? What do you think it was all about?'

'I've no idea, David. It could have been all manner of things. In the middle of the night funny things happen, and even normal, rational people don't behave rationally at dead of night! You're the creative one... Whatever you dream up as the reason behind the call would probably be easier to believe in than the true reason!'

So David took his leave, content that he had police approval to give free rein to his imagination, went home and spent the rest of the day listing possible scenarios for him to work on. At the end of the day he had on paper the outlines of at least ten situations which, he told Margaret later, might be capable of being transformed into stories.

'Only might?' she asked.

'Yes, until you really get down to the actual writing bit, you can never be absolutely sure that an idea is going to work!'

'Well, you know what to do about it, don't you?'

'No, but I know what you're going to tell me to do about it though!'

'And what's that?'

'Just get on with it!'

'Okay, so do it!'

'It's not quite as straightforward as that!'

'Why not? You said yourself that you've already got ten outlines of situations in mind, so where's the problem?'

'I'll tell you where the problem is – it's inside my head.'

'Then get it out and talk about it! That's what we've always done before when you feel that your train has run into the buffers! And we usually find that the solution is inside your head too... So tell me what you see as a problem...'

'Shall I lie down on the couch?'

'If you like, but I'm not a very good psychiatrist. I usually just listen...'

'That's what good psychiatrists do, isn't it?'

'Up to a point, I suppose. Anyway, tell me what appears to be the problem.'

'I'm a writer of short stories.'

'Yes, I know that, but why is that a problem? It's never stopped you writing before.'

'It's a problem because what I'm working on now is a novel, not a short story...'

'Go on...'

'And my plan so far is to invent ten or so explanations for the mystery phone call...'

'True...'

'But don't you see, if I do that, I shall have ten or so short stories...'

'Yes...'

'So I will still be a writer of short stories, not a novelist!'

'Does it matter?'

'Yes, I think it does. I think there is a difference between a collection of short stories and a coherent novel.'

'Which is?'

'There needs to be a unifying factor somewhere, something to pull it all together.'

'There is.'

'So what is it?'

'The unifying factor is the phone call.'

'I know that, but I don't think that's enough. I've racked my brains to see if I can find a way to have a character, or some characters, reappearing in every story, so that it's always, for instance, the same person who makes the phone call, or the same person who receives the phone call, but I can't see a way to do it. In fact, the more I think about this project, the more I think it's a dead duck!'

'I'm sure it isn't! There has to be a way round it!'

'Well, I can't see it!'

'Hang on a minute! I think I can...'

'Go on then.'

'You want an overall theme that embraces the whole book, okay?'

'Yes, exactly.'

'Well, I think maybe it's staring us in the face.'

'It is?'

'Maybe... Try this for size... You've already got a short-story writer who wants to be a novelist, haven't you?'

'Yes.'

'And you've got the initial situation – what we called the 'hook' when we first started talking about it... And then this brilliant writer of short stories dreams up a series of stories each explaining how that mysterious phone call came about...'

'Yes.'

'But then he realises that a series of short stories isn't enough to make it into a novel...'

'That's exactly my point.'

'And so you stop bottling up all the problems you're having and put them into the book properly...'

'I don't quite see...'

'What I mean is that the phone call isn't the unifying factor – or rather, it isn't the only unifying factor – the overall unifying factor is the transformation of the writer of short stories into a novelist...'

'Oh, I see what you're driving at now! Brilliant!'

'In other words, any difficulties the writer comes across, he talks to his wife about – which is what you and I always do anyway – and now, instead of fretting about it and allowing it to prevent you writing, you just make it an integral part of the story.'

'Do you think I need to change the names then?'

'I don't think you should use our real names, no, not our surname anyway! How about David and Margaret?'

'I think that will do very nicely, darling!'

Chapter Two

Every day for the next two or three months, David made at least half a dozen attempts to contact the person who had called him in the night, so concerned was he for the mental health of the caller, and so worried was he about the situation, whatever it was, which had led somebody to get in touch with the police, but the result was always the same: the number remained 'unobtainable'.

Although he had been re-living the incident constantly, and diligently attempting to find logical explanations for what had happened, he still felt that he was nowhere near finding out the truth. So he continued to worry, he continued to try to explain it, and he continued to call that number.

But even ringing a number unsuccessfully half a dozen times a day does not take up a great deal of time, and after his wife had challenged him to transform his worrying experience into a book, David sat at his computer the very next morning and started to write. The following day he did the same, and the next, and the next... By the end of the week he not only had one story finished, but he printed it off and presented it to Margaret. 'Well done,' she said, 'I really didn't think you would get this off the ground!'

'Oh ye of little faith! Why on earth not?'

'Because you didn't seem too sure of your ground, and I'm not used to seeing you short of confidence in your writing.'

'I'll have more confidence if you're convinced by the first story!'

'So all I've got to do is say I don't like it, and that will scupper your ambition for ever, do you mean? That's an awful position to put me in, I must say!'

'No, I don't mean that! Obviously I'd like you to like all my stories, but I really need a genuine opinion, I don't want you to tell me you like it if you think it's awful!'

'You know me better than that! Okay, give me the story and I'll read it after supper this evening.'

'Okay, here you are.'

So, true to her word, immediately after supper she began reading – while her husband washed the dishes; and this is what she read:

'Did you enjoy that, darling?' said Ben after they had finished eating. 'And how about coffee and a liqueur?'

'Oh yes, it was a really lovely meal, Ben,' said Sylvia, 'but what say we have coffee and liqueurs when we get home rather than having them here? Then we can just tumble into bed whenever we feel like it...'

'Good idea!' Ben responded, secretly more motivated by the thought of tumbling into bed with Sylvia than by the idea of coffee and liqueurs by the fireside. 'I'll ask the waiter to bring the bill right away.'

Ben gestured to the waiter, who immediately moved to the till and printed off the bill before coming over to their table.

'I hope you enjoyed your meal, madam,' the waiter said as he approached the table.

'Yes, very much,' Sylvia replied, 'very much indeed. We'll certainly come again.'

'Is this the first time you've dined here?'

'Yes, it is. Actually we don't often eat out these days, except on special occasions.'

'Oh... and is tonight a special occasion then?'

'Yes, it is, it's our Silver Wedding...'

'Congratulations, madam, and congratulations to you, sir.'

'Thank you,' Ben mumbled impatiently, still thinking of the warmth of their bed. 'Do you think you could call us a cab?'

'Of course, sir, no problem.'

The waiter handed the card machine to Ben, then, once the transaction had been completed, returned to the till and picked up the phone. One minute later he was at their table again. 'Your cab is ordered, sir. It will be here in two minutes.'

Ben and Sylvia got up from the table, and, by the time the waiter had retrieved their outdoor clothes and they had put them on, they saw a taxi draw to a halt outside the restaurant. Once in the taxi Ben told the driver the address, and he and Sylvia settled comfortably into the back seat, as the taxi made its way up The Promenade in the direction of Leckhampton.

'What a lovely evening it's been,' said Sylvia to Ben, 'thank you so much, darling!'

'It has been a nice evening, hasn't it! I'm so glad you enjoyed it. I'm always a little bit wary of going to a newly opened restaurant, particularly when we're celebrating something special!'

'I know what you mean,' Sylvia replied, taking Ben's hand and squeezing it affectionately.

'Maniac!' shouted the taxi driver suddenly. 'Bloody hell! Did you see that?'

'No,' said Ben, 'I'm afraid I wasn't watching. What happened?'

'Some blithering idiot totally ignored a red light and came charging out of Oriel Road straight in front of me and disappeared up St George's Road. I was lucky not to crash into him! Look, there he is again! Oh God, he's just demolished a traffic bollard too!'

Ben looked out of the car window and saw a distinctive looking orange mini careering erratically up St George's Road.

'Good God!' Ben exclaimed. 'Look at that, Sylvia! I'm positive that's Roy's car! Driver, stop please! I need to go and see if the boy who's driving is all right.'

The driver pulled up as soon as he could, and parked at the side of the road. 'Do you mean you know the driver of that car, sir?'

'Yes, of course I do. It's my son!'

Ben jumped out of the taxi without waiting to hear the driver's caustic comments on his son's competence as a driver, and ran into St George's Road, but by the time he reached the damaged bollard, the orange mini had disappeared into the distance – as far as he could see, without any further misadventure. In consequence there was nothing Ben and Sylvia could do, other than get back in the taxi and continue their journey back home.

Once they had returned home, however, Ben lost no time in ringing his son's number, with Sylvia sitting beside him with bated breath, but there was no answer, even though the number he had called was that of his mobile, which normally accompanied him everywhere, and which he appeared to use all the time.

'What the devil was he playing at!' exclaimed Ben in exasperation. 'And where the hell has he gone to now? He certainly wasn't going home, he was driving in the wrong direction! I expect he had a girlfriend in the car, and he's taken her home... Do you know who he's going out with now?'

Sylvia laughed. 'I have absolutely no idea,' she said. 'I just can't keep up with him! Since he ditched that lovely girl Marilyn and left her to go and live on his own he must have had at least half a dozen girl friends!

Goodness knows why he dropped Marilyn. I really thought that was going to be a long term relationship...'

'So did I,' said Ben, 'she was a bit of all right, was Marilyn.'

'Well, he obviously didn't fancy her as much as you did!'

'Ha, ha!' Ben replied sarcastically. 'Do you want a proper conversation about this or not?'

'Of course I do! You were the one that started fantasising about Roy's former girlfriend, not me!'

'Actually,' said Ben, ignoring his wife's teasing comment, 'although you said that it was Roy who dropped Marilyn , I'm not so sure that it was Roy who initiated their break-up.'

'Oh, do you know something that I don't then?'

'I doubt it! You usually know far more about this sort of thing than I do! But I do remember two or three times while they were living together when he intimated that Marilyn was giving him a bit of a hard time.'

'Oh, that was just because she was getting fed up with Roy being away from home so much, that's all!'

'Well, if you make your living working as a rep, that's what you do! She knew it would be like that before she moved in with him! Did she say anything to you about it?'

'No, in fact I don't know any more than that, it was just an impression I got, nothing very concrete.'

'But then there was something a bit more serious later on, wasn't there?'

‘Was there? I didn’t know about anything else. Roy never said anything to me about it anyway.’

‘There was one evening when I went for a drink with Roy, and while we were in the pub, he told me how much he would like to have children...’

‘Oh, I didn’t know anything about that.’

‘Well, I don’t know a great deal about it really, but I got the impression that Marilyn didn’t want any.’

‘While they were still unmarried, you mean? I can understand that...’

‘No I think she told Roy that she didn’t want any ever! I would have thought they needed to get things like that sorted out before they started living together, don’t you?’

‘You may be right, who knows! I always think it’s impossible to judge other people’s relationships, but everybody seems to do it all the same! But, frankly, all that’s immaterial, the relationship’s all over, and we need to think about Roy’s physical well-being right now. Driving like that indeed! Roy is clearly not safe to be at the wheel of a car at the moment, is he?’

‘No, you’re right, he isn’t. I’ve never seen driving like it!’

‘So what are you going to do about it?’

‘Why me?’

‘Because you’re supposed to be the action man!’

‘Ha, ha! Very funny! I propose to do nothing at this precise moment, but as soon as you’ve finished making funny remarks, I think we should call the police.’

‘Do you really think that’s a good idea?’

'I don't know. I don't really want to get Roy into trouble, but he obviously shouldn't be behind the wheel at the moment, and, since we have no idea of his whereabouts, the only people we can turn to are the police. Did you see the way he demolished that bollard? It's just as well it wasn't somebody crossing the road that he hit. It's a question of public safety. I don't want him to finish up killing somebody! He would have it on his conscience for the whole of his life!'

So Ben rang the police and told them about his son's reckless driving, adding details about the make and registration number of his car and his address, but making it clear to them that he would be unwilling to give evidence in any prosecution that they might bring, because he hadn't been with him, that he was not in possession of all the facts, and that his principal concern was public safety.

In the meantime Ben and Sylvia's son Roy was making his way home to his flat in Charlton Kings, having just dropped off his companion for the evening at her home on the other side of Cheltenham. He had just passed through the town centre and noted that the bollard that he had demolished on his outward journey was still lying in the middle of the road, when he became aware of a flashing blue light being reflected in his rear view mirror. He glanced at his speedometer to check that he was complying with the 30 mph speed limit, but the police car, now immediately behind him, started flashing its headlights in an obvious signal to the driver of the car they were following that they wanted him to stop.

Roy, however, satisfied that he was driving legally and convinced that the car the police were chasing could not possibly be his, kept on driving, whereupon the police car suddenly accelerated and overtook Roy's car, swinging round and coming to a screeching halt just in front of him. Roy was thus forced to perform an emergency stop, and only narrowly managed to avoid smashing into the side of the police car. Two policemen immediately jumped out and walked round to speak to Roy, who wound down the window.

'Would you mind blowing into this, sir?' asked one of the policemen, holding out a breathalyser.

'Why should I?' Roy asked.

'Because we say so,' came the reply.

'I don't think that is sufficient grounds,' Roy argued. 'I wasn't over the speed limit, I didn't drive through a red light or anything like that. I think you'll find the law says that I need to have done something like that to be breathalysed.'

'Oh, God, we've got one of those,' one of the policemen muttered, whilst his colleague continued the conversation.

'I know the law, sir,' he said, 'and it also says we can breathalyse you if we have reasonable grounds for suspecting that you are over the drink-drive limit.'

'And do you have reasonable grounds?'

'Yes, sir, I believe we do.'

'And those grounds are?'

'You were seen earlier colliding with a traffic bollard in St George's Road.'

'By whom? Did you see me?'

'No, not personally, but we had a report to the effect that this car was being driven erratically before it demolished a bollard.'

'So if you didn't see me personally, how do you know that I was driving at the time?'

The police officer ignored the direct question and asked one of his own. 'So you deny that you were in collision with a bollard, do you, sir?'

'If you didn't see me do it,' said Roy, deliberately dodging the question, 'I would like to see what evidence you have. What time was this collision supposed to have taken place, by the way?'

'About half an hour ago. So where have you been this evening?'

'Why should I answer that question?'

'Because if you don't, I shall charge you with obstructing the police in the course of their duties, sir. I advise you to answer our questions.'

'Why?'

'If you haven't done anything wrong you have nothing to fear,' said the policeman.

'Oh yes? I've heard that before,' Roy scoffed.

'Oh, so you've been in trouble with the police before, have you? When was that?'

'I didn't say I had been in trouble with the police.'

'You implied you had.'

'In your mind!' Roy replied scornfully.

'So where have you been this evening?'

'I don't see why I should answer that question!'

'In that case, would you mind accompanying me to the station?'

'Is one of you planning to get a train?'

'Very droll, sir. Let me put it this way: you can choose to answer my questions here, or to accompany me to the police station, where somebody else will ask you the identical questions.'

At last Roy realised that he had no alternative but to answer, so he replied, 'I've been out to a restaurant with my girlfriend.'

'That's better, sir. Which restaurant?'

'The Balti in Rodney Road.'

'And where's your girlfriend now?'

'At home, I suppose.'

'When did you last see her?'

'When I took her home.'

'Where does she live?'

'On the Hester's Way estate.'

'And what's her name?'

'Marilyn Booth.'

'And her actual address?'

Roy provided him reluctantly with Marilyn's address.

'Was she with you when you smashed into the bollard?'

'I didn't say I had smashed into any bollard. You said that...'

'So I did,' the policeman admitted with a sigh. 'Now at the restaurant, did you have any alcohol?'

'A glass of wine.'

'Just the one, sir?'

'The waiter may have topped it up when it was half empty, but I didn't have any more after that.'

'And was your girlfriend drinking?'

'Yes, she had a lot more than me, but she wasn't driving.'

'Was she aware that you'd driven into a bollard?'

Roy was once more careful to dodge the leading question and replied, 'I doubt very much whether she was conscious of anything! She was probably asleep.'

'Because she'd had too much to drink?'

'I didn't say that. She was tired.'

'And you?'

'What about me?'

'Did you drop off at the wheel? Is that perhaps why you collided with a bollard?'

'I didn't admit that I had collided with a bollard, so you're wasting your time trying to make me agree that I did! And I certainly did not drop off at the wheel. But if you carry on like this much longer there's a chance I shall drop off on the way home, because I'm getting tired of this!'

The policeman took no notice of Roy's taunt, and said, 'All right, off you go! But we shall follow you home, and if we see you driving recklessly, we won't hesitate to pull you in. Understood?'

'Understood.'

'Good night, sir.'

Roy ignored what he interpreted as the policeman's tactical switch to a polite manner, switched on the engine and drove off, taking care to do nothing that might tempt the policemen to intervene once more. As they had promised, the patrol car stayed with him until he parked his car outside his flat, and it was not until he was safely inside the house that the police car finally moved off.

Once he was back home Roy made himself a cup of coffee and sat down for half an hour before preparing to go to bed, for he had much to think about – not so much about the police, more about Marilyn, for his former girlfriend had dropped a veritable bombshell that evening.

It was the first time Roy had met Marilyn for about two months, for Marilyn had unilaterally declared that their relationship was going nowhere, and that they should stop living together. But a couple of days ago, a letter from Marilyn arrived out of the blue, suggesting to Roy that they should meet, because, she said, she needed to talk to him.

'Well, if you hadn't refused to make a note of my new mobile number when I offered, we would have been able to talk straight away,' said Roy to himself. Then he turned his attention once more to her letter, in which Marilyn had said that what she needed to tell him could not be communicated by letter, and proposed instead that they go out for a meal and have what she described as a 'civilised chat'. 'I suppose she would also pretend that whatever she wants to talk about is not something she could talk about on the phone either,' Roy commented sarcastically to himself.

It took two or three weeks to set up the meeting that Marilyn appeared to consider urgent, because of the current nature of the postal service; if only Marilyn had been willing to call him on his mobile, Roy thought, it could all have been arranged in a matter of minutes.

They met in an Indian restaurant in the centre of Cheltenham. In the event, although the evening began in a civilised way, things deteriorated fairly rapidly. The downturn started with Roy asking what she wanted to tell him that could not be explained in her letter.

'Let's order first,' she replied, 'it's not the sort of thing I'd like anybody to overhear.'

Although Roy was beginning to think that he would never get to learn the urgent news that Marilyn kept saying she needed to tell him, he acquiesced, and a few minutes later, once the waiter had brought their food and moved away from the table, Marilyn decided it was time to make her announcement, which, to Roy's surprise, was only two words long.

'I'm pregnant,' she said.

'Oh?' replied Roy.

'Is that all you have to say?' Marilyn demanded.

'What do you expect me to say? It's nearly ten weeks since we stopped living together, so the baby can't possibly be mine, and if I'd asked you who was the father, you would have told me to mind my own business!'

'Quite right too,' came the rejoinder, 'but what makes you so sure that it's not yours?'

'As I said, we haven't even seen each other for ten weeks, so it can't possibly be mine!'

'All right, clever clogs, but I went to see the doctor yesterday, and he says I'm at least three months pregnant, and, by my reckoning, "at least three months" is a lot more than ten weeks!'

'I'll grant you that, but why does that prove that I'm the father?'

'What the hell are you suggesting?'

'I'm not suggesting anything. I just want proof, that's all.'

'So you think that while I was living with you I was also seeing someone else, do you?'

'How should I know?'

'Because I'm not that sort of girl!'

'If you're not that kind of girl, why did you walk out on me? I still don't know why! You never gave me any explanation of any kind, so I naturally assumed that you'd found somebody else.'

'Well I hadn't!'

'So why did you walk out on me?'

'I didn't walk out on you! You were living at my place, remember, so how could I have walked out on you. I didn't!'

'No, and if it had been left up to me, I wouldn't have left! I certainly didn't walk out on you! One day, quite out of the blue, you told me to move out, and that was that! And you never even told me why.'

'You never asked...'

'I bloody did! Several times.'

'Don't swear! People are looking...'

'I'm not surprised! So why exactly did you decide one day to tell me to leave?'

'Because our relationship wasn't going anywhere.'

'You were wrong then!'

'What do you mean?'

'I mean you're wrong to say that our relationship wasn't going anywhere! After all, if we're going to have a baby, our relationship certainly is going somewhere, isn't it?'

'What do you mean?'

'Oh, come on! It stands to reason, if you're going to have a baby and you say the baby is mine, we're going to be the baby's parents, aren't we? And being parents is a bit different from being boyfriend and girlfriend...'

'I suppose it is, if you put it like that...'

'Well look, I didn't want us to break up in the first place; it was your idea, not mine! And if you're really having my baby, I want you to know that I'm willing to do the honourable thing.'

'Which is?'

'Oh God! I'm just trying to make it clear to you that I'm willing to marry the mother of my child!'

'I'm sorry, but I don't want you to!'

'You what?'

'I said I don't want you to.'

'So why did you tell me?'

'Tell me what?'

Roy sighed. 'Why did you tell me you're having my child?'

'Because I thought it was the decent thing to do. I'm having a baby, you're the baby's father, and I thought I should tell you.'

Roy reached across the table to place his hand on Marilyn's, but she withdrew it at once.

'What's the matter?'

'You seem to have got the wrong end of the stick, Roy! Because I thought it was the right thing to do to tell you that I was pregnant, that doesn't mean that I want to force you to marry me!'

'I didn't say anything about force! I'm willing to. I want to!'

'I'm sorry, but I don't! I'm perfectly capable of bringing up a child on my own...'

'But you don't need to!'

'I want to! I don't need you! A woman doesn't need a man! And I don't want you either!'

'I thought you told me that the child is mine. How can I be a child's father if I don't have a hand in bringing him up?'

'You've done your bit, and that's as far as it's going, Roy! And that's my last word.'

'But it's not my last word! What do you mean by saying that I've done my bit?'

'Exactly what I say. You've had your bit of fun, and now that's over.'

'I never heard you complain at the time!'

But Marilyn persisted in saying nothing, so Roy continued, 'Is that all you've got to say?'

'Yes, I told you I wasn't saying any more. Please take me home.'

'I will when I'm ready! I think you've got a nerve!'

'What do you mean?'

'You start a relationship and give me the impression that you're as happy as I am, and then, without even suggesting that you're unhappy, you chuck me out! And then when you find you're pregnant, you get in touch and tell me – not because you want me back, but so that you can watch me squirming with pain as you twist the knife!'

'It isn't like that at all!'

'It is from here, I assure you! And I find it difficult to believe that you're contemplating looking after a child all on your own when it's not exactly a hundred years since you told me emphatically that you didn't want children anyway!'

'A girl can change her mind, can't she? It's probably something to do with the way a woman's hormones react when she does become pregnant...'

'I wouldn't know about that...'

'No, of course, you wouldn't, would you...'

Roy argued some more, but however hard he tried, he was unable to make her say anything other than that she didn't need him and didn't want him, so he settled the bill and they both left the restaurant and walked to the nearby car park, where they both got into Roy's mini, which was the signal for hostilities to resume, on a much more bitter basis too, now that they no longer had any potential eavesdroppers. As they drove past Cheltenham Town Hall they were both screaming at each other furiously, and Roy swerved violently to avoid colliding with a taxi.

'Be careful, you fool!' Marilyn shouted. 'You just went through a red light! I'm so frightened! Slow down, for God's sake!'

Roy's response was to accelerate as they entered St George's Road, so Marilyn screamed again, 'I've had enough of this! I'm getting out!'

Still screaming, she began to open the passenger door, whereupon Roy turned to look at her and, taking his eyes off the road, but still driving too fast, proceeded to demolish a traffic bollard in the middle of the road.

After that, neither of them said another word until they reached their destination, although Marilyn spent the rest of the journey sobbing uncontrollably. As soon as they reached her house she opened the car door, and ran to the house without a word. By the time Roy got out of the car she had disappeared into the house. Roy walked up to the house, tried the door, then rang the doorbell, but the door remained stubbornly closed, so he returned to the car, got back into the driving seat and started to make his way home.

Unbeknown to Roy, as soon as the policemen had finished interviewing him, they then drove straight to Marilyn's house, where they rang the bell. They had more luck than Roy had done, for Marilyn actually answered the door, whereupon they informed her that Roy's father had been in touch with them and suggested that his son had been driving recklessly, and they spent the next sixty minutes interrogating her before going on their way. In truth they learnt nothing significantly new from Marilyn, who spent most of her time trying to ensure that her replies to their questions did not incriminate her, for she was well aware that Roy's erratic driving had been caused more by her own hysterical behaviour than by his negligence – in that she had suddenly opened the passenger door and threatened to jump out while they were doing at least 30 miles an hour through the centre of Cheltenham! It was no more than an accidental by-product of this that led to her not giving the police any evidence detrimental to Roy.

Although Marilyn had actually had rather less wine at the restaurant than Roy had given the policemen to believe, once the officers had taken leave of her she did indeed open a bottle of white wine and, within a matter of seconds was already on her second glass, as she went over in her mind the events of the evening, in particular her conversation with Roy.

At length, at some time between one and two o'clock in the morning, she started to worry that Roy might think that she herself had got in touch with the police. The more she thought about this, the more she became convinced that she must let him know that she had not been responsible for the police involvement. But on what number should she contact him? She had not phoned him in the two months since he had moved out; even when she wanted to suggest that they might meet that evening to talk things over, she had written him a letter because she did not know his telephone number, and for the previous two years she had not needed to call him because they had been living under the same roof. Eventually the thought occurred to her that his number would probably be in one of her old diaries, which she kept in a drawer in her desk, so she went to look and, sure enough, she found the one which referred to the year before he had moved in with her, and there she found his name and two telephone numbers, one for his mobile and one for a landline. A moment's thought made her ignore the mobile number, for she recalled his having told her he had changed his mobile phone a couple of months previously, so she found herself, shortly after two o'clock in the morning, dialling the number of his landline.

She heard the number ringing out, but for what seemed to be an age there was no answer, so she poured another glass of wine. Still the tone continued sounding. She had another drink. Then, at last, she heard a man's voice at the other end of the line, a voice which lacked clarity, which seemed full of sleep – which should not have been surprising to her given the time, but she was beyond rational thought by that stage.

'Hello,' she heard.

'Can you hear me?' she asked.

'Yes,' a man's voice answered.

'Are you listening?' she continued, but for what seemed like an eternity there was no answer.

'Are you listening?' she asked again.

'Yes, I'm listening,' said the voice.

'This is very important,' she said very slowly and deliberately. 'I did not call the police. It was your family who called the police.'

'What? What are you talking about? What do you mean? I don't know what you're talking about...'

She ignored his protestations and hung up, satisfied that she had done all that was necessary to salve her conscience; if Roy did not understand what she was saying, she thought, that was his problem, not hers.

She finished off the bottle of wine and took herself to bed, where she slept for at least ten hours, for it was lunchtime before she was able to force her eyes to open sufficiently wide to be able to see the clock.

At about the time when Marilyn was climbing drowsily out of bed, Ben was telephoning his son Roy, for he still had not spoken to him about what he and Sylvia had observed from the taxi the previous evening.

'Hello, Dad,' said Roy as soon as he picked up the phone.

'Hi Roy,' said Ben, 'how on earth did you know it was me?'

'Oh, I've got caller identity on my new phone.'

'You've got what?'

'Caller identity.'

'What's that?'

'Oh, it's just a facility on my new mobile which displays the number of the person that's calling you when it starts to ring.'

'So it shows you who's calling before you answer?'

'Yes. It's quite useful really, because it enables you to decide whether you want to answer the phone or not. If the phone rings and I don't recognise the number that comes up, I tend not to answer.'

'That sounds useful. We have so many calls these days from people who want to sell us double glazing, or insurance, or God knows what else! And it might have enabled me to avoid a phone call I had about two o'clock this morning! But I suppose I would still have been woken up when the phone rang!'

'Who was it?'

'I don't know! I suppose it was someone who dialled the wrong number. But whoever it was, she was talking a lot of nonsense!'

'You didn't recognise her voice?'

'No. That is, it did seem vaguely familiar, but I couldn't place it.'

'What did she say?'

'She asked me if I was listening, because it was very important. Then she said, "I did not call the police. It was your family that called the police."'

'What did you say?'

'I told her I had no idea what she was talking about, but she had already rung off by the time I said that.'

'So you never found out who she was?'

'No, I didn't, but it was so obviously a wrong number that I just put it out of my mind and went back to sleep. Talking about phone calls, I tried to call you last night, but you didn't answer.'

'No, I was out last night.'

'Anywhere nice?'

'Not bad. We went to an Indian restaurant in Rodney Road.'

'Who's we?'

'Oh, I went out with Marilyn.'

'Marilyn? I didn't think you were still seeing her....'

'I wasn't, but she wanted to talk, so we went out for a meal.'

'And are you back together?'

'No, we aren't, there's no chance of that.'

'Oh, that's a pity, I liked Marilyn.'

'I used to.'

'Oh, I see. That sounds pretty final.'

'Yes, I think it is.' Roy thought of telling his dad what they had been discussing, but decided it was not something he wanted to discuss at the moment, and in any case not over the phone.

'That's funny,' said Ben. 'It's just occurred to me whose voice that woman on the telephone reminded me of – it sounded a bit like Marilyn. But of course it couldn't have been.'

'No, of course it wouldn't have been,' replied Roy, who was less convinced than he sounded. 'Anyway, Dad, I've got to go out. I'll give you a call a bit later on, or else tomorrow, okay?'

'Okay, Roy,' said Ben, as he put down the phone.

Roy sat down and thought about the conversation which he had just been having with his father, for there was something at the back of his mind which was making him feel uneasy. He took out his phone again and dialled Marilyn's number.

'Hello,' she said.

'Hello, Marilyn, it's Roy.'

'Hi, Roy,' she said. 'Are you still mad with me?'

'What do you mean?'

'Well, you were furious with me last night, so I was just wondering if you still felt the same today.'

'I'm not still angry, no, but I still don't understand you. As I said last night, I would still be willing to marry you.'

Marilyn completely ignored his answer and pressed on.

'Have you spoken to your family this morning?'

'Yes, I've just been speaking to my dad. Why?'

'Did he talk about the police?'

'What about the police?'

'You know, last night... I told you when I rang you last night...'

'But you didn't ring me last night. We went out to a restaurant, don't you remember?'

'Of course I remember, but no, it was after that. It was in the middle of the night that I called you.'

'You didn't call me in the middle of the night! The last time I spoke to you was when I dropped you home after we'd been to the restaurant. You ran into the house and bolted the door! I rang the doorbell goodness knows how many times, but you still wouldn't open it! If you'd really had something to say to me, it might have been better to open the door! What time did you ring?'

'I don't know exactly, but I suppose it was about two o'clock or something like that. It was well after the police came to see me, I know that.'

'The police came to see you? What about?'

'About your driving.'

'What about my driving?'

'When you drove me home from the restaurant you were driving erratically, they said, and you demolished a traffic bollard. They told me that they'd been talking to you about it.'

'Yes, they stopped me on the way home from your place. Then they asked me where I'd been and who with, and made me tell them where you lived.'

'I'm sorry about that.'

'It wasn't your fault. I wanted to keep you out of it, but they insisted.'

'I was afraid that you thought that it was I who had reported you to the police. That's why I called you late last night.'

'Yes, you said that before! But you didn't call me last night!'

'I did!'

'What time?'

'I've already told you! I don't know exactly what time it was, but I suppose it must have been about two o'clock.'

'I was asleep at that time! I obviously didn't hear the telephone.'

'So why did you answer it?'

'Answer it?' Roy questioned incredulously.

'Yes, that's right.'

'So what did I say?'

'Not very much at all. You sounded as if you were still asleep.'

'I'm not surprised! I was! I can assure you that I didn't speak to you or anybody else once I got home. I had a coffee and then went go bed.'

'Well, somebody answered my call, so who could it have been?'

At last Roy spotted a glimmer of light at the end of the dark tunnel. 'Well, tell me this – what number did you actually call? A few months ago, when I changed my mobile, I offered to tell you my new number, and you said you didn't want it, so it couldn't have been on my mobile!'

'No, it wasn't on your mobile, because I didn't know your mobile number! It was on your landline.'

'But I don't have a landline. When I moved into my new place I decided it wasn't worth bothering with a landline, because I'm out a lot, and even when I'm at home, I always have my mobile with me. I suppose you looked in the phone book and saw somebody with the same surname, did you?'

'No, I found your number in one of my old diaries.'

'Oh, I understand now. For you to have my landline number in your diary, it must have been a diary dating back to before we started living together! That must mean that you called my parents' house! I suppose you didn't say to the person who answered, by any chance, that you didn't call the police, it was their family that called the police, did you?'

'Yes, that's exactly what I said! So, if you didn't get my call, how do you know what I said?'

'Because my dad told me.'

'Your dad?'

'Yes, my dad! You were searching for a number in an old diary, and you found what used to be my number when I was still living with my parents! No wonder my dad was mystified!'

'I'm sorry about that. I thought I was talking to you...'

'But you weren't.'

'I know. I'd had a lot to drink last night.'

'You didn't have a lot at the restaurant!'

'I know I didn't, but after I got home I did. I needed to steady my nerves after you'd driven me home.'

'Why?'

'You ought to know! I've never been so scared in a car before!'

'It was your fault!'

'How could it have been my fault? You were the one who was driving! You even knocked down a traffic bollard!'

'Only because you said you were going to jump out of the car!'

'I was only kidding!'

'Only kidding! So why did you start to open the car door?'

Marilyn refused to admit that she had opened the door while Roy was driving, so Roy changed the subject.

'But I want to talk about our baby,' he said. 'You were obviously embarrassed about discussing it in the restaurant last night, even though you were the one that brought it up. You had told me there was something we needed to talk about, and suggested spending the evening together, and when I asked you what your news was, you told me you were pregnant, and we never got to the point where we had the 'civilised conversation' that you said you wanted!'

'Well, I'm not.'

Roy could not believe his ears. 'You're not what?'

'No, I'm not pregnant.'

'So why did you say you were?'

'To see what your reaction would be.'

'And what was my reaction?'

'You said you wanted to marry me.'

'So why was that the wrong reaction?'

'I'm not the marrying kind. And I didn't think you were either.'

'Why not?'

'You never suggested marriage even while we were living together, not even once!'

'Neither did you, by the way!'

'I told you I'm not the marrying kind. Do you have a problem with that?'

'Not in itself. But I wouldn't care to be married to a wife that's a liar.'

'I'm not a liar! How dare you?'

'Well, last night you told me you were pregnant. This morning you're telling me you're not. So you were either lying last night or you're lying this morning. Which is it? No, on second thoughts, don't tell me, I don't care any more! You don't want me, and now I've seen what you're really like, I don't want you either! Goodbye!'

With that he switched off his phone, and immediately went out to make his peace with his parents and explain to them the mystery of the phone call they had received at dead of night.

As soon as he had typed the words, 'the mystery of the phone call they had received at dead of night', David printed off the story and handed it to his wife.

'I'll read that straight after lunch,' said Margaret.

After lunch Margaret took David's typescript into the conservatory and read his story; as soon as she had finished she went to David's study and told him she'd read it.

'What did you think of it?' he asked anxiously.

'I think it's very good,' she said, 'but I'm not sure I understand the girl's motivation...'

'You mean Marilyn? I don't think she understands it herself. She's quite a mixed up girl!'

'You can say that again! But it doesn't quite ring true to me. She informs Roy that she's pregnant, and when he tells her he's willing to marry her, she says she's not the marrying kind. I wouldn't react like that!'

'But you're of a different generation, and you *are* the marrying kind, thank God! And you wouldn't have dreamt of telling me you were pregnant if you weren't, would you?'

'No, I wouldn't dream of it! I can't understand it. She's a nasty piece of work, that girl!'

'Yes, I think she's a nasty piece of work too. You're not suggesting that I shouldn't have any characters in my stories who aren't purer than the driven snow, are you?'

'Certainly not! I wouldn't think of saying anything of the sort! But if she had gone to live with Roy and stayed with him for two years, why on earth would she suddenly have kicked him out?'

'Because she's basically self-centred.'

'But it's not even in her own interests, is it? I suppose there might be some women who are as self-centred as that, but I can't think of any that I know!'

'I'm not sure I know any either, but what does that matter? Look at it this way: an author has to invent characters of a type he's never come across in real life. Quite a few of my stories have involved murderers, haven't they? And as far as I know, nobody of my acquaintance is a murderer. I hope you're not saying that if I don't know any murderers I shouldn't have any in my stories?'

'No, of course not!'

'Thank God for that! I'd hate to be limited to inventing characters who resemble people I know! As it is, the idea for that story came to me after I'd been talking to George Smithers at the tennis club a couple of weeks ago. He told me that his daughter-in-law had just kicked out her husband after more than ten years of marriage, because she wanted to live her own life and she didn't need him any more.'

'Do they have children?'

'Yes, I think they do.'

'That's appalling!'

'I think so too, but it's the sort of thing that can happen sometimes these days. They call it empowerment. They believe that women don't need men.'

'That's not empowerment! Empowerment is to do with preventing women being subservient.'

'I know that, you know that, but not everybody does! There are obviously some women who are fundamentally selfish, and who use the notion of empowerment in order to indulge their own selfishness. Not everybody is as good-natured as you are!'

'Flatterer! Okay, I agree, you can have nasty women in your books, as long as you don't have any in your life! But there's something else that's bothering me a bit about that story too...'

'What's that?'

'Oh, it's only a little thing. If Roy's car really had collided with a bollard, the car would bear some marks, wouldn't it?'

'Yes, I suppose it would.'

'But the policemen didn't have a look at the car to see if it was marked, did they? And yet they went to all sorts of lengths to get him to admit that he had collided with a bollard!'

'You're assuming that all policemen are as intelligent as you are! And, as I found out when I phoned the police station last Saturday morning, there are some policemen who are a couple of sandwiches short of a picnic! And in any case, an author isn't obliged to put every minute detail into his story. As you say, the author is God!'

Chapter Three

The following Monday morning, David got up very early with a view to starting work on creating his next story, his wife Margaret being still in bed. At 7.30 he took a cup of tea up to her, and then went on to complete another half-hour's work before going to get dressed, after which they had breakfast together.

'You got up very early this morning,' said Margaret. 'That doesn't happen very often these days!'

'Yes, I know,' replied David. 'I was often in the habit of getting up early to work when I was a bit younger, but I seem to need more sleep these days! But for some reason this morning I woke up at about five o'clock and then something in my brain started thinking about my book, and after that I couldn't get back to sleep again, so I eventually decided to get up and use whatever useful ideas popped into my head.'

'And did any?'

'One or two....'

'Were they good ones?'

'I don't know yet. But probably the most significant thing is that I decided in particular that in the different scenarios I invented I didn't necessarily have to maintain consistency from one story to the next.'

'What do you mean?'

'What I mean is, that it doesn't always have to be someone who sounded like the man's daughter that was making the call. It could be somebody who had a similar speaking voice to the man's wife, girlfriend, ex-wife, or whoever. In fact I went as far as thinking that the voice of the caller doesn't even have to sound like that of somebody the man knew anyway. And then although the original call to me came to our landline, it could just as easily have been on my mobile...'

'Frankly, all that doesn't sound particularly significant to me. Does it really matter?'

'Not a lot, no, only insofar as it would make things a lot more difficult for me if I had to maintain exactly the same situation from one scenario to another. In fact it probably wouldn't matter to the reader at all, but to the writer it would! Because, of course, the really important thing is that the message has to be identical each time. You see, when I had the original call, it was the nature of the message that started to get under my skin, it didn't have anything to do with the fact that it was on our landline, or even because I had been under the impression that the call came from Susan...'

'I see... so do you think you have made much progress?'

'Well, yes, I think I have, because I've done a lot of thinking about the whole situation this morning, and there are a few ideas buzzing around my head which weren't there last night. So, although I haven't actually put a lot of words down on paper this morning, I'm at least in a position to make a start!'

'Jolly good! So when do you expect to finish the next instalment?'

'In theory I should have finished it by Friday. But there's a lot of work to do between today and then!'

'Well, you'd better get on with it then. Off you go!'

So David went off to his study, and then on Friday afternoon he handed the next instalment to Margaret, and this is the story she read:

Michael Davenport lived with his wife Janice in Bromley, Kent, in a neighbourhood which was effectively a suburb of London, even though it was nominally in the county of Kent. Nobody could have claimed that their marriage was a happy one. In fact the prospects had been at best uncertain in the first place, because they had both been married unhappily before, but each of them had believed that this time they would be able to make a go of it. Almost immediately after their wedding, however, the squabbles started: fairly trivial and insignificant to begin with, but in time progressively more serious, until, after a couple of years of bickering, it became obvious to everybody, and to each of them, that the marriage was doomed, and they both stopped trying, without actually having a proper conversation about it, which is probably the real reason that the marriage was so unsuccessful: each of them was content to leave the outcome to chance, without putting any genuine effort into it themselves.

The problem had started, in Michael's opinion anyway, because their three children did not hit it off at all, especially the two girls. None of the children was actually the result of their union: when they married, Michael's daughter Angela was fifteen, almost the same age as Janice's daughter Jane, and a year younger than Jane's elder brother Graham. The way Michael viewed the situation was this: Jane, who had initially been enthusiastic about her mother marrying Michael, and who had appeared to be on good terms with Angela at that time, had begun to resent her stepsister, criticising her stepfather for always tending to favour his own daughter. She also began to accuse her brother Graham of making up to Angela, although he, a fairly equable young man, was by nature the sort of boy who tried to get on with everybody. Janice's view, however, was almost the opposite of Michael's: according to her, it was Angela who was being unkind to Jane, and who, from the very beginning, had resented any show of affection between her father and her stepmother into the bargain. The irony of this situation was that if Angela and Jane had been just friends, they would in all probability have been the best of mates.

It would, of course, have been better if such misunderstandings – if misunderstandings they genuinely were – had been identified and sorted out before the wedding, but at that stage Michael and Janice only had thoughts for each other, with the children being left to cope with their new situation as best they might, and neither husband nor wife appeared to notice the early signs of imminent disaster, and when eventually they did become aware of their children's deeply felt resentment, they both made the fatal mistake of taking sides. Within two years, however, both Michael and Janice were involved in extra-marital affairs, a situation which was facilitated by the fact that Michael often had to be away on business. He was area manager for a big company manufacturing washing machines and other 'white goods', and frequently had to confer with and assess the work of his team of local agents; to begin with, Janice felt that he arranged to be away from home rather more than was strictly necessary, but, once she had established her own liaison, she ceased to complain about his absences, because the fact that he was often away made it easier for her to do as she liked.

It soon became apparent, however, that Michael was totally incapable of making an illicit relationship last any longer than a marriage, and, after three or four affairs which each failed within two or three months, he settled for a series of one-night stands, mostly involving young women who worked for the same company, and of whom he was at least nominally in charge. Many of them appeared to believe that it would be a good career move to make up to their regional boss; the fact that most of them were married women did not seem to matter a great deal, either to him, or, in his own mind at least, to them.

On one occasion Michael was due to visit the Lake District, which involved a much longer drive than usual, so he booked into a little hotel just outside Keswick; the next day he was due to spend the morning with the local rep, a young woman named Tracey Bannister, whom he had not met before. Tracey also had a relatively long drive, because she lived in Southport, not too far from Liverpool, and the only civilised way she could arrive in Keswick by nine in the morning was by travelling the day before and staying overnight. Michael had helpfully suggested that it would be more convenient if they stayed at the same hotel, and that if they had dinner together, they would be able to get to know each other more quickly, and make the most of the time they would be spending together – for the ultimate benefit of the company, of course...

Michael arrived at the hotel at about five o'clock in the afternoon; he went straight up to his room, unpacked his overnight bag, had a shower and a shave, and generally made himself more presentable. A few minutes later his mobile rang: it was Tracey letting him know that she too had just arrived at the hotel, and that she was in a room on the second floor.

'I'm on the first floor,' Michael declared. 'because I always like to be within easy reach of the bar. Do you want to come down to my room, or shall I come up to yours? I've been looking forward to meeting you face to face!'

'Shall we just meet in the bar? Say in fifteen minutes?' she replied guardedly.

If Tracey had been able see Michael's face she would have noticed immediately that disappointment was written all over it. But he was a man who believed his charms were irresistible, so he reluctantly accepted a short delay. 'Okay,' he replied, 'in fifteen minutes I shall be in the bar.'

A little less than fifteen minutes later Michael left his room and made his way to the bar, but when he arrived he found there was no woman sitting on her own – in fact there were no women in the room at all. He chose a table at a reasonable distance from the bar and an equal distance from the door, so that he would be able to see his employee as soon as she made an appearance; from that position he would also have time to assess his tactics as she crossed the room. Immediately a waiter appeared at his table, so he ordered a bottle of *Prosecco* and two glasses.

'Shall I wait until the lady joins you?' asked the waiter.

'No,' said Michael, 'I'm dying for a drink! I'll have it straight away.'

'Very good, sir,' said the waiter obediently, and in a couple of minutes he returned with a bucket of ice in which the bottle had already been placed, and two empty flutes; at once he poured a glass for Michael, then withdrew, whereupon Michael immediately started drinking.

It was fully five minutes before Tracey made her appearance. When she did, she looked around the bar, and seeing there was only one man sitting alone, she made her way towards Michael's table; as he had planned, he had ample time to inspect her before she arrived in front of him. She was in her early thirties, had shortish blonde hair, blue eyes, and was wearing a deep blue trouser suit and a white sweater which showed off her figure to advantage. 'Oh yes,' Michael thought, 'I like the look of that. It might be my lucky night!'

'Are you Mr Davenport?' she asked as she approached his table.

'Michael, please!' he pleaded. 'We're off duty now, we can let our hair down a bit! Come and sit down, Tracey...'

As he spoke he pulled out a chair for her, choosing the one nearest to his seat, but, without saying anything, she pulled out a chair for herself – on the opposite side of the table from Michael, and sat there. 'Oh, champagne!' she exclaimed, 'I love champagne!' Despite her enthusiastic words, she was in fact feeling a little disappointed, for it had not escaped her notice that the bottle contained *Prosecco*, not genuine champagne, which would have cost him – or, more accurately, the company – about four times as much; she was equally conscious of the difference in quality, as well as the attitude it implied.

'Only the best is good enough for my staff!' he announced pompously as he poured out a glass for her, whilst she simply offered him a smile by way of thanks. 'I always think of my team as being my family. So welcome to my family!'

'Your family?' she questioned, listening properly for the first time, and rather surprised by the expression.

'Yes... I mean welcome to the team!' he said, raising his glass, 'I hope you'll be very happy working for the company. If there's anything you need, please feel free to ask.'

'Thank you, Mr Davenport,' she replied, raising her glass in turn, and taking a couple of sips from it before replacing it on the table.

'Call me Michael,' Michael reminded her. 'And tell me about yourself.'

'Oh, there's not much to tell,' Tracey replied. 'I live in Southport, I've only just joined the company, and before that I was working for a bank.'

'How long were you working for the bank?'

'Almost exactly two years.'

'And why did you leave the bank?'

'I found it boring sitting there at the counter day in, day out. And when I saw the advert for this job, I thought I'd rather like travelling to different places.'

'Are you married?'

'Yes, I am.'

'Children?'

'Not yet.'

'How long have you been married?'

'Just coming up to three years.'

'What does your husband do?'

'He's in the army.'

'Does that mean he's away a lot?'

'Sometimes. He's in Iraq at the moment.'

'How long has he been away?'

'Eighteen months so far.'

On hearing this, Michael felt encouraged, assuming immediately that the fact that her husband was serving abroad must mean that she was pining for male company, especially since, in addition, they had been separated for half of the duration of their marriage. 'That must be lonely for you,' he commented. 'And Southport's not exactly the liveliest place I've ever visited.'

'Oh, do you know it then?'

'Not very well, no, but I have played golf at the Royal Birkdale a couple of times. Do you play golf?'

'No, not at all. Was it Mark Twain who described golf as a perfect way of ruining a good walk?'

'I haven't heard that before, so I don't know who said it. But whoever he was, I don't think he was right. I find golf gives me a lot of pleasure and plenty of exercise too.'

A slightly awkward pause followed, which Michael filled by topping up Tracey's glass and then emptying the remains of the bottle into his own glass, for he had already drunk a glass and a half himself before Tracey's arrival. 'Waiter!' he called, 'another bottle of this, please!'

'Steady on! You'll get me tipsy!' Tracey said.

'And what if I did?'

'I don't know.'

'I'm sure a lovely girl like you must have been tipsy now and again!'

'I might have done!'

'And what happened?'

'I can't remember. But excuse me, I need to go to the Ladies' Room.'

'Okay. I'll be right here.'

So Tracey made her way out of the bar, returning two or three minutes later. But when she returned to the table where Michael was sitting, she noticed that, instead of four chairs, there were now only two at the table, of which one was occupied by Michael, with the remaining one having been placed much closer to Michael than it had been before.

'Oh!' she exclaimed, 'somebody's moved the chairs!'

'Yes,' said Michael in a matter-of-fact way. 'The bar's been filling up, and the waiter came and asked if we really needed four chairs. Naturally I said no, and so he took the two that were nearest him. You don't mind, do you? I mean, we don't really need four chairs, do we?'

'Oh no, of course not!'

Tracey discreetly looked around her and noticed that the neighbouring table had six chairs, none of them occupied; so much for it being necessary for the waiter to move chairs, she thought. Despite the obvious signs that she needed to be cautious, she sat down on what was now the only vacant chair at their table, just alongside the chair occupied by Michael; it was then that she noticed their bottle of sparkling wine had been replaced and that both their glasses were once more full.

'Here's to us!' said Michael, raising his glass.

Tracey did not reply, but she responded by raising her own glass too, and had two or three more sips before replacing it on the table. It was then that she realised that Michael's hand was now resting on her thigh.

'Do you mind?' she said, removing his hand from her thigh, and feeling relieved that she had chosen to wear a trouser suit rather than a short skirt.

'Not if you don't!' said Michael, deliberately taking her answer the wrong way.

'I'm a married woman!' she protested.

'And I'm a married man,' Michael admitted.

'What would your wife say if she knew what you were doing?'

'I don't know, but if she'd seen what a pretty girl you are, she would probably express her surprise that it had taken me so long!'

'And you mean she wouldn't mind?' asked Tracey incredulously.

'She wouldn't mind at all! What's more, when I get home tomorrow, I wouldn't dream of asking her what she's been doing tonight!'

'Why's that then?'

'Because I expect she's been taking advantage of the fact that I'm away overnight.'

'Do you mean she'll be with another man?'

'I expect so, yes.'

'And don't you mind?'

'I suppose I did at first, but eventually I got used to it. And it means I have a free hand when I'm away.'

'Yes, I noticed that you were fairly free with your hands...'

'Ouch!'

'Does it hurt if I make comments like that?'

'Not really. I was just joking.'

'So what do you want from me? Do you want to get me into bed?'

'Yes, please!'

'Well, I'm sorry, but the answer's no!'

'Why?'

'Because I hardly know you!'

'You soon would!'

'I'm not sure I want to. Let's get this straight. Do you mean my job depends on going to bed with the area manager?'

'No, of course it doesn't!'

'So I'm free to say no, am I?'

'I thought you already had done!'

'And that makes no difference?'

'Well, I'm very disappointed, and I hope you'll reconsider. Would you like another glass of wine?'

'Do you think another glass would make me change my mind?'

'It might!'

'And it might not!'

'I'll take a chance on that! But I really would like you to change your mind.'

'Why?'

'Isn't it obvious? Because I'd like to make love to you...'

'But why?'

'Why does any man want to make love to a woman?'

'I don't know. You tell me...'

'Because he thinks she's nice-looking and he fancies her something rotten!'

'That's lust. You said you wanted to make love to me!'

'What's the difference?'

'Lust is purely physical. Love implies tenderness...'

'And how do you know I wouldn't be tender to you? I'll be as tender as you like!'

'No, you won't!'

'How do you know that?'

'Because you won't get a chance. You won't get anywhere near my bed!'

'Have another drink...'

'No, thank you. I think I've had enough. If I hadn't, I wouldn't be having this conversation with you either!'

'Oh go on, we could have a lot of fun...'

'You might, but I certainly wouldn't! The answer's no, and the answer's going to remain no! I'm going to bed – and you're not invited!'

Michael tried to delay her departure, reminding her, for instance, that they hadn't yet had anything to eat, and in fact they continued wrangling for another half hour, but Tracey's answer was still no, and finally she managed to escape to her room, and, she believed, relative safety. But Michael was not easily deterred, and it was not long before she heard a tapping at her bedroom door, which she greeted with a cry of, 'Go away, Michael, I'm going to bed – on my own!'

After a while, however, she started to feel distinctly peckish, and she contacted Room Service to order a sandwich. Even so, she had not yet succeeded in ridding herself of Michael's attentions, for when her sandwiches arrived, he was still lurking in the corridor just outside her bedroom door.

Even after that she found the telephone ringing every quarter of an hour or so, but she decided to ignore it, convinced that it was Michael, a suspicion that was later confirmed when her mobile too started to ring, and this time, of course, her phone revealed the identity of the caller. Still the calls continued until just after midnight, at which point Michael appeared to have got the message at last, for the calls ceased.

When he eventually went to bed, Michael went straight to sleep rather than fretting about his inability to persuade Tracey to share her bed with him, but he had, of course, had quite a lot to drink over the course of the evening, so that is not particularly surprising. It was not very long before he was awoken once more, however, for the phone starting ringing at about two o'clock.

He reached out to answer the bedside phone, said 'Hello', but there was nobody on the other end. It was only when he became conscious that a phone was still ringing that he realised that he had answered the wrong phone: the call was on his mobile. His first thought was that Tracey might have changed her mind and was about to invite him to join her, but when he picked up the mobile he found that the call was from a number that he did not recognise. Even so, he accepted the call and said 'Hello?' once more.

'Are you listening?' said a woman's voice which sounded rather familiar, but which he could not place.

'Yes,' he replied automatically.

'This is very important,' said the voice. 'I did not call the police. It was your family that called the police.'

'What on earth do you mean?' he demanded, but there was no reply, for the caller had terminated the call.

Despite the enigmatic nature of the message he had just received, Michael was soon fast asleep again, for he had been too full of alcohol to take in much of what was happening, and the next thing he knew, there was somebody hammering on his bedroom door. He looked at the clock and saw that it was seven o'clock. He dragged himself out of bed, put on his dressing gown and went to open the door. There he found himself being confronted by a policewoman in uniform, and two men in civilian clothes. 'Are you Michael Davenport?' the policewoman asked.

'Yes, I am,' he replied. 'What do you want?'

Michael's three visitors held up their warrant cards, to indicate that they were all members of the police force, and one of the men said, 'I am Detective Inspector Clarke, this is Police Sergeant Williams, and this is Policewoman Buchanan. We are investigating some allegations of sexually inappropriate behaviour.'

'What has that got to do with me?' asked Michael, puzzled.

'That's exactly what we want to find out,' said the inspector, 'and another colleague, Policewoman Bannister, will be joining us in a moment – oh, here she is.'

Michael's eyes followed the direction in which the inspector was pointing, and, to his utter amazement, he saw Tracey coming towards them. What's more, she too was brandishing a police warrant card, and holding something in her other hand which looked like a mobile phone.

'I think you know Policewoman Bannister already, don't you, sir?'

'I didn't realise she was a policewoman though,' Michael growled.

'I suggest that we move into your room, Mr Davenport, unless you would like our conversation to be overheard by the general public.'

Michael nodded, and they all went into his room, whereupon the Detective Inspector continued: 'We would just like you to listen to this, Mr Davenport. Go ahead, Policewoman Bannister.'

Tracey flicked a switch on the little tape recorder she had been holding in her left hand, and this is what Michael heard:

'Yes, I noticed that you were fairly free with your hands...'

'Ouch!'

'Does it hurt if I make comments like that?'

'Not really. I was just joking.'

'So what do you want from me? Do you want to get me into bed?'

'Yes, please!'

'Well, I'm sorry, but the answer's no!'

As Michael heard his own words and Tracey's responses being replayed to him, he went pale.

'Are you denying that that is your voice and that of Policewoman Bannister?' said the inspector.

'No, but I didn't realise she was a policewoman.'

'Would it have made any difference, sir?'

'Yes, of course!'

'Why?'

'I would have known better than to say something like that to a policewoman!'

'I don't believe it should make any difference! To be honest, it doesn't sound to me like the sort of thing you should be saying to any woman! Would you like to hear some more? We've got the whole conversation…'

'No, I don't want to hear any more. This is entrapment, that's what it is!'

'I don't think so, sir. Especially not when we're responding to a number of complaints.'

'What complaints?'

'Complaints from girls who were afraid they'd lose their jobs if they didn't accept your lewd propositions!'

'What girls?'

'You'll find out when we get back to the station, sir.'

'But I've got a business appointment at 10 o'clock. I can't go to the station!'

'Yes, you've got an appointment with Policewoman Tracey Bannister, haven't you? She'll be there at the station too, don't worry, so you won't miss your appointment!'

'I think your policing methods are disgraceful, inspector!'

'And I think the way you treat your female employees is disgraceful too, sir, but I don't expect you will agree with me!'

'It's only her word you've got to go on though, isn't it?'

'No, it's not. You heard yourself part of the recording she made, and she recorded the whole of the conversation. We have statements from some other young women too, and they all report remarkably similar conversations to the one that Policewoman Bannister recorded last night.'

'Oh, do they really? And how many statements do you reckon you've got?' Michael asked defiantly.

'Eight.'

'What did you say?'

'I said we have eight, sir. There are eight women who have submitted complaints to the company, which is why they called us in.'

'That's a bit underhand, I must say! Why didn't the company ask me about it before calling the police?'

'Because of the seriousness of some of the charges, sir. They include three accusations of rape.'

'Rape? I've never raped anyone in my life!'

'The conversation Policewoman Bannister recorded last night tells me you had rape very much in mind! And that would have made four.'

'That wouldn't have been rape! Rape is violent! I wouldn't have been violent. I wouldn't have hurt her. That was the last thing I had in mind!'

'Rape isn't necessarily violent, sir, it's simply a question of insisting on having sex when the woman has said no. Now would you say, Mr Davenport, that you would have taken any notice if any of these girls had said no to your sexual advances?'

'Of course I would! But of course a lot of girls say no at first! And then they usually change their minds when you get started!'

'Oh, do they, sir? I wouldn't know.'

'Look, Inspector... These girls work for me, I regard them as my family... I wouldn't hurt any of them!'

'Your family, eh? I seem to have heard that expression before somewhere. Play your other recording, Tracey.'

Policewoman Bannister pressed the switch on her recorder again, and Michael heard the words he had heard in the night: 'This is very important. I did not call the police. It was your family that called the police.'

Michael turned to Tracey and said, 'I thought that voice sounded familiar! But I didn't recognise your mobile number when I accepted the call, and I never dreamed it was you!'

'I have two mobiles. And no, you wouldn't have recognised my voice because you hadn't been listening to me properly, had you, right from the very beginning? But then you never listen to anything a young woman says, do you, especially when she says no!'

'I didn't mean you any harm, Tracey! Please believe me!' Michael pleaded with a whimper.

'Just get some clothes on, Mr Davenport, and we'll go down to the station,' said the inspector. 'And you may make one phone call before we go. I suggest you call your solicitor.'

'Can I call my wife too?' asked Michael.

'Frankly, I don't really recommend your calling your wife, sir, because I don't think you'd find her very sympathetic. We've already spoken to her, so she does know all about it, and, off her own bat, she said she wouldn't have been a bit surprised if you had raped all those girls. Come on, get dressed and we'll be off.'

'I think I'd like to speak to her even so,' replied Michael, whereupon the Detective Inspector relented, and allowed him to make two calls before leaving the hotel. He contacted a lawyer first, then called his wife.

'I thought you'd be the last person I would hear from this morning!' she said, on hearing his voice. 'Have you heard anything from the police?'

'Yes, they're here now, and they said I could phone you if I wanted.'

'I'm surprised you wanted to speak to me, given what you've been up to! But I'm glad you did call, because I wanted to tell you that when you come home I shall only allow you into the house to collect your belongings. This is the last straw, Michael, and I'm going to divorce you!'

'Oh, please, Janice, don't do that! What shall I do?'

'You can do whatever you please,' she replied. 'I don't care what you do! I'm sure one of those floozies you've been hob-nobbing with for God knows how long will take pity on you! But I certainly won't! I've had enough!'

'I'm sorry, Janice,' Michael began to say, but she cut him short.

'I just can't understand how I was taken in by a man like you! You're disgusting!'

'Just tell me this,' Michael pleaded. 'How did you know that the police were involved?'

'Because they came to see me.'

'When?'

'Last Friday.'

'But that was before I even came up to the Lake District! Why didn't you say anything about it to me?'

'Because the police told me not to, because they were planning to set a trap for you, I suppose, and they didn't want to ruin their chances of catching you. I don't blame them either! You're an absolute rat!'

'Do either of our girls know about it?'

'Not at the moment, no. But I expect they will do soon, because if there's a court case, there's going to be a lot of publicity, and they're bound to find out! I just hope you haven't tried it on with either of them! Have you?'

'How can you even think of asking a question like that! Of course I haven't! I'm not that sort of man.'

'What sort of man are you then? A pretty disgusting one by the sound of it! How could you treat all those young girls like that! I can't bear to think about it! There's only one thing you've ever been interested in as far as women were concerned, and that's self-gratification. Goodbye! This is the last time you'll ever speak to me.' Then she put down the phone.

As soon as Michael had finished speaking to his wife, the door opened, thc Inspector reappeared, and saw Michael in floods of tears.

'I told you I didn't think it was a good idea of yours to ring your wife, didn't I?'

'Yes, I know, but I didn't expect anything quite like that! She even went as far as to suggest that I might have interfered with my daughters...'

'I'm not surprised either, sir, given what you have been up to!'

'But I wouldn't have done anything to them! Oh, God, what have I done with my life!' And he started crying again.

'Come on, sir. I've got to take you to the station.' And Michael, still in tears, meekly accompanied the policeman out of the hotel, was pushed roughly into the police car, and they drove to the station.

At the police station Michael was led into an interview room where he waited alone for half an hour until his solicitor arrived, after which DI Clarke and Policewoman Buchanan joined them and the interview began – such as it was, for, following the advice of his solicitor, Michael answered hardly any of the questions asked. So Inspector Clarke read out to him extracts of the statements made by some of the women who had complained about his behaviour, and then formally charged him with having raped three women and having sexually assaulted five others; in the afternoon he appeared at Keswick Magistrate's Court. Given the seriousness of the charges he was remanded in custody awaiting a County Court appearance. Within half an hour he received a phone call from his boss informing him that he had been dismissed from his job; three months later he was sent to prison for five years.

'Well,' said Margaret, when she had finished reading David's latest story, 'I wasn't expecting anything like that! What an odious character he turned out to be! Still, I suppose there must be some people like that in the world. But I didn't expect that when I started reading the story — he came across as a pleasant, very affable character!'

'Well, yes, of course he did,' replied David, 'I should imagine anybody who behaves like he did would normally give a good first impression, otherwise all those women wouldn't be taken in by him! I mean, if slimy, odious characters gave themselves away at first glance, they wouldn't get anywhere, would they?'

'I suppose not,' said Margaret, 'but how did you come to dream up a story like that? It sounded so authentic – I suppose you've never tried to seduce a woman in that way, have you?'

'I expect my solicitor would advise me to refuse to answer a question like that!' said David, laughing. 'But I do have a good imagination – otherwise I wouldn't be able to be a writer! And when you come to think of it, I've written loads and loads of murder stories, but you've never suspected me of being a secret assassin, have you?'

'I suppose not,' replied Margaret, 'but then I've never met a murderer!'

'How do you know? Murderers, rapists, blackmailers, confidence tricksters, they must all depend on presenting a respectable front to their victims. That's one reason why their crimes are so odious!'

'I guess you're right! But that's quite a worrying thought – I may never trust anyone who's outwardly respectable again!'

'Quite right too!' replied her husband.

'And now I expect you're going to start planning your next story – I hope it doesn't worry me as much as that one did! Promise that it won't!'

'I have absolutely no idea what it's going to involve,' said David, 'you'll just have to wait and see! You were complaining that I'd invented a nasty woman for last week's story, and so this week I chose to invent a nasty man, just to keep the balance! The important thing is whether the story does its job, and fits in with the set of imagined scenarios...'

'Oh yes, it does that all right, it's very convincing. And I like the variation on the phone call as well – it was quite ingenious to have it coming from a member of the police force too!'

Chapter Four

On the first day of the following week, David began work on his next story. As they had breakfast, Margaret said to him, 'What are you planning to write about this week then?'

'I have absolutely no idea,' he replied.

'Really?'

'Really! I haven't even started to think about it!'

'But you told me when you first started on this project that your mind was absolutely full of ideas!'

'So it was! But sometimes, when you start examining what appeared to be a promising idea for a story, you find that your idea doesn't really work.'

'Does that mean that you abandon that idea altogether, then?'

'No, not at all! In fact I often revisit ideas that I've abandoned a couple of weeks or so ago, and I find out that, with a little tweak here or there, I'm able to make it work after all! Do you have any ideas for a new story yourself?'

'Good God, no! The very idea! I thought you realised a long time ago that I'm one of the least creative of beings!'

'There are times when I think that's true of me too! But that doesn't mean that it is the absolute truth. It's often just a question of application – you apply the seat of the trousers to the seat of the chair and the ideas come flooding in! That's what I'm hoping will happen this morning! It's always been the same when I'm starting a new story. Right up until the time that I sit down, open my notebook and pick up my pen, I feel terrified that this time I shall be devoid of inspiration, and then hey presto! I start writing and the words just flow, as if they're coming from nowhere!'

'Then let's hope it continues to work!' said Margaret.

'Too true, but I live in dread that it might not! It always has so far, but I have no right to believe that it always will!'

'Is that why you always seem slow to get down to work on a Monday then?'

'That's not true! I don't think I am!' retorted David, who went on to remind her that on the previous Monday he had got up particularly early, and did some significant work before breakfast. 'Anyway, if you don't mind clearing away the breakfast things, I'll crack on.'

'I beg your pardon? I was under the impression that that is what happens every morning!'

'You must be joking! I clear up after breakfast at least half the time! Anyway, everyone is entitled to believe their own illusions, I suppose, so I won't argue – I've got too busy a morning ahead of me to sit around arguing about clearing the breakfast table!'

Margaret's response was to screw up a paper serviette and throw it playfully at her husband's head.

'Ha! You missed!' he said teasingly.

'I missed on purpose! I wouldn't like to risk damaging those delicate little brain cells of yours! They are going to have to focus on higher things,' said Margaret laughing, as David made his way to the study.

Once seated at his desk, David picked up his pen, applied the pen to the paper, and, to his intense relief, the words did come pouring out.

Des Wilson had been a long-distance lorry driver for just over thirty-five years. He had passed his basic driving test at the tender age of seventeen, then joined a road haulage firm in Canterbury, his home town, initially as a tea boy and a general dogsbody, but, even as a boy, he had always had an eye on becoming one of the drivers.

He had had to wait for four years to achieve his dream, however, because of his age: at that time the minimum age to hold a licence to drive Heavy Goods Vehicles was twenty-one. But that was all long in the past: he was now in his early fifties and was by far the most experienced of the firm's drivers.

He would have been the last to claim that the romance of being a long-distance international lorry driver had worn off, yet these days he always breathed a sigh of relief when he arrived home safely, and the truth is that he was not one of those men who worry intensely at the very notion of impending retirement: the thought of sitting around at home with nothing to do held relatively few terrors for him, because he had many interests and considered that anyone who was bored had something fundamentally wrong with them.

He certainly still enjoyed driving on the continent, deriving much pleasure from the comradeship which existed among the lorry-driving fraternity, at least among the older members; the younger ones, he felt with some regret, had a tendency to regard every trip as just another job, and they always seemed to be dying to get back home, instead of making the most of the opportunity to experience the rich tapestry of Europe's many cultures.

Not for them the pleasures that Des had enjoyed most, of spending evenings abroad eating and drinking with fellow drivers, from whatever country, and relatively few of them had Des's inclination to learn enough French, German, Spanish and Italian to be able to converse and to enjoy the company of the men who were his companions every evening he was on the road. He was not really a linguist, but he had learned to communicate rather more effectively than many who had spent a long time in the classroom.

But in every country of Europe, it seemed, the older drivers were gradually being replaced by the young, who appeared to have a quite different mentality and were less inclined to be sociable in their leisure time when they were abroad. Des himself blamed the invention of the mobile phone for that – what was originally meant to be a highly useful invention had, in his opinion, mutated into a slave driver, and most of the young truckers, as they had started to call themselves, seemed to spend their mealtimes communicating with people at home, whether sending or receiving texts, or actually speaking to people at home, and thus ignoring completely everyone who was sitting at their dining table.

There had been a further change. Since the turn of the millennium, cross-channel lorries had regularly been targeted by would-be immigrants to Britain, but in Des's heyday there was one phenomenon which had been virtually unknown to everyone, and totally unknown to him: stowaways.

But one day, in the Spring of 1979, he was on the way back from a routine trip to Spain: having delivered a load of packaged medicaments and car parts to Barcelona, he was returning with an enormous load of Spanish tomatoes.

It was a journey that Des used to undertake fairly regularly in the 1970s and 80s. It was just a little too far for a lorry driver to drive legitimately from Barcelona to Calais in one day, so Des usually chose to have a break at a *Relais Routiers* just outside Reims, a place favoured by many of his fellow lorry drivers because they could be assured of eating well there, and in good company too. This allowed him also a fairly leisurely drive to Calais the next morning, after which he would drive onto the ferry and have a decent meal and a rest before tackling the short journey from Dover to Canterbury, where he would arrive in mid-afternoon.

On this particular occasion he made his way into the restaurant at Reims to find a number of his acquaintances already at the table and engaged in a conversation which appeared to be even more lively than usual, but not lively enough to prevent them from greeting him warmly and making a place for him.

'So what's going on?' he asked in French. Such was the cosmopolitan nature of the group that he was not particularly surprised to find his question being answered in Spanish.

'We're talking about hitchhikers,' said the Spaniard, whom Des had known for a year or two, and whose name was Miguel. 'But not the sort of hitchhikers we're used to having – these are not ordinary young people, they are not students, they are young families: mother, father, and two or three kids.'

'That's unusual,' said Des, 'I don't think I've ever had children in my cab before.'

'That's what we were just saying when you just came in,' said a German named Kurt. 'We've all got used to picking up the odd student off on their holidays, but these people are intent on getting into Britain and never coming back.'

'That's all right if they come from the European Community, isn't it?' said Des.

'But that's just the point,' said Kurt. 'These people aren't. They're usually from a country which is outside the European Union, like Romania or Bulgaria, which means that, unless they're just on holiday, they are bound to be classed as illegal immigrants.'

'But if they're already in France,' said Des, 'they're illegal immigrants here as well, which means that if there is a problem, it's the responsibility of the French government to deal with it. But have any of you picked any of them up yet?'

'No,' said an Italian named Giovanni, 'precisely because they generally want to go to Britain, and most of us European drivers stay on this side of the Channel. In any case, they prefer British drivers, because they feel they are more likely to be able to help them once they get into England. What about you, Des, would you be willing to give them a lift?'

'I don't know,' replied Des. 'It would depend.'

'It would depend on what?' asked Kurt.

'It would depend on what their story was,' replied Des.

'I'll tell you their story,' said Kurt, 'because it never changes. If they're Romanian, which they usually are, they will say that they are tired of living in a Communist dictatorship, especially under a leader like Ceausescu. They will say they have no money and they want to live somewhere where their little kids will have a better life.'

'And is their story true?' asked Des.

'Sometimes, but sometimes not,' said Kurt.

'Well, I wouldn't pick up any of them,' said a Frenchman named Pierre, who had not yet contributed anything to the conversation. 'It's asking for trouble to pick them up. They're illegal, and that's enough for me! They're criminals. The police should arrest them, and, like Des said, it's the responsibility of the French government, so I can't understand why the French police don't do something about it!'

'But what if these Romanians have small kids?' asked Giovanni. 'From what I've heard, some of them even have babies with them! Surely babies can't be criminals!'

'No, but the parents are!' Pierre insisted.

'Is it fair to punish a little baby because his father is so desperate that he's willing to break the law in order to give his baby a chance of a better life?' asked Giovanni.

'No, it's not,' said Des firmly. 'There are too many people suffering in the world as it is. I'd be willing to take someone with a baby.'

Des's response had the effect of making all the company start talking at once, and the fact that they were all speaking in their native language made their conversation seem even more chaotic. All of a sudden, the incongruity of it all made someone start laughing, and, before long, peaks of laughter started ringing throughout the room, as usually happened at that time in the evening, at the point where tiredness, wine and their natural garrulousness combined. 'It's time for bed,' said Des, 'I'm off! See you all soon! Bye!'

Cries of '*Arrivederci*,' '*Au revoir*', '*Hasta luego*' and '*Auf wiedersehen*' greeted Des's words, and he went up to his room, where he was soon fast asleep.

The following morning he got up at about seven, had breakfast, and went down to his lorry at about 8.30. Just as he was unlocking the door of his cab, he heard a voice behind him. 'Please can you help me, sir?'

He turned round and saw a young woman holding a baby, who could not have been more than a few months old.

'How?' he asked. 'What can I do for you?'

'Is this your truck?'

'Yes.'

'Are you going to England?'

'Yes.'

'We are going to England also, but we have no money. Can you help us?'

'What do you mean?'

'Can you take us in your lorry?'

Des looked at the young woman. She was probably not even out of her teens, she was pretty, but shabby and ill-kempt; her baby was wrapped in a tattered shawl and had no shoes. 'Yes, all right, I'll take you,' he said.

'Can you take my husband also?' the young woman asked.

Des followed the direction of her eyes and saw a young man, not much older than the girl and equally shabby, who was standing holding two little toddlers by the hand. 'Oh, I didn't realise you weren't on your own,' he started to say, but one look in the direction of the little family melted his heart. 'Oh, all right,' he said, 'I'll take you.'

Because Des did not speak a word of Romanian, he motioned to the young man to climb into the cab, and directed him, again by gesture, to occupy the middle of the bench seat, then passed the baby to the father and helped the toddlers and their mother into the lorry too; once they were all safely installed, he went round to the driver's door and climbed in himself. Very soon they were en route, and in no time at all his passengers were, without exception, fast asleep.

They remained asleep until after Des had parked his lorry in the car park just in front of the entrance to the ferry port in Calais, and even then he had to wake them up, wondering, as he tried to rouse them, when they had last profited from a good sleep like that. Once the parents were awake, he said to them, 'We're just about to board the ferry, and you'll need to show your passports.'

His statement was greeted by a look of horror on the face of the young man. 'But we have not passports,' he said.

'None of you?' he asked.

'No. In Romania it is only the very rich who have passports, and we are not rich. We are ordinary people, and ordinary people are not allowed to have passports. That is why we ask you to take us.'

Des looked at his watch and saw that in just five minutes time the barriers would be closed and they would all miss the ship. 'All right,' he said, 'there's only one thing to do. You will have to hide in the back of the lorry, but it will be very cold in there. I have two blankets that I can lend you, but you will need to hide until we are on board the ship.'

He was particularly worried by the fact that his lorry was towing a refrigerated container: necessary if you are carrying a load of tomatoes or pharmaceutical supplies, but not recommended for the well-being of a human being, let alone a little baby, even for a short time.

In a matter of minutes he was driving his lorry onto the ship; he had done the trip so frequently over so many years that most of the port employees, including the French policemen and the customs officials, were on first name terms with him, and those who did not know him personally tended to be juniors, being supervised by an older man who had known Des for several years.

Once on board the ferry, Des went up to the lorry drivers' canteen, where, even though he had eaten a hearty breakfast already, he bought a number of croissants and baguettes; no one seemed surprised, or even questioned his apparently Gargantuan appetite, because the long-distance lorry drivers had a continent-wide reputation for being able to consume a quantity of food before which a lesser man would quiver. Unusually, however, he returned to the vehicle deck and made his way back to his lorry, and opened the rear doors. At first he was not able to locate his secret passengers, but he soon found that they had made their way as far from the rear doors as possible. 'Are you all right?' he asked the young mother.

'Yes,' she replied, 'it is cold, like you said, but we are used to being cold.'

'Is Romania a cold country then?' asked Des, 'I've never been there.'

'Every country is cold if you have no home,' said the man.

'I expect you're hungry as well as being cold,' said Des. 'So I've brought you some food and some water,' he continued, showing them the croissants, the bread and some bottles of mineral water; the delight which spread across the faces of the little ones when they saw the food was so tangible that Des at once lost any qualms he might have been harbouring.

'Thank you, thank you!' said the adults, 'You are very kind! Thank you!'

'Not at all,' replied Des. 'The happiness on the face of those children is thanks enough.'

The parents, however, continued expressing their thanks; not so the children, however, for they were too busy eating – at first, anyway, although the oldest child, whose name Des discovered later was Ion, eventually mumbled something which resembled '*Merci*', which led Des to ask Ion's mother if her little boy spoke French.

She looked puzzled at his question, and replied, 'No. Why you think so?'

'I thought I heard him say thank you in French.'

'Ah, I see,' she said with a smile, 'the Romanian for thank you is usually *multumesc,* but very often Romanian people say *merci* if they want to say thank you. The Romanian language is very close to French, and to Italian too.'

'So, if I spoke in French to your husband would he understand?'

'Yes, but Italian would be better. Marius speaks Italian.'

'Marius?'

'My husband. His name is Marius.'

It was not until that moment that Des realised the significance of the name of his new friends' native country; Romania had at one time been a Roman province, and had maintained its name. So Des addressed Marius in Italian, and was delighted to find that Marius's answer was easy to understand.

From that moment onwards the conversation between the two Romanians and their host was free-flowing, despite switching unpredictably from Italian to French, from French to Romanian, and then back from Romanian to Italian again; it was just like having dinner with his fellow truck-drivers, Des thought.

During the remainder of their sea voyage, Des was able to discover that Marius's surname was Petrescu, and that his wife's name was Ana Maria; their children were Ion and Cristina, whilst the baby was called Elena. Marius, it transpired, was a lawyer in Bucharest, but he had decided to leave his native land because his outspoken attitude towards the regime of the Romanian President Ceausescu had come to the attention of the *Securitate,* the state secret police, as dreaded in Romania during Communist days as the *KGB* in the Soviet Union and the *Stasi* in East Germany.

Ana Maria, however, was more interested in finding out about Des and his family than in speaking about the stressful circumstances which had led to their leaving Bucharest. So she came to learn that Des was married to Thelma, that they had no children, although they would love to have had some of their own. Des, however, experienced such difficulty in trying to explain in Italian that the development of *in vitro* fertilisation had come too late to be of any use to them, that he did not even attempt to explain that the reason why they had not followed the alternative route of adoption was because at that time all the adoption agencies were run by the various churches, and anyone who, like Des and Thelma, were not themselves regular churchgoers, would stand virtually no chance of adopting a child. Even so, bit by bit, a genuine *rapport* was being established between this humble lorry-driver and his would-be illegal stowaways.

Suddenly Des spotted one or two lorry-drivers starting to return to their lorries, signalling that the ferry was approaching the port of Dover, whereupon he instructed Marius and Ana Maria and their children to return from the driver's cab where they had been sitting chatting to Des, to their hiding-place in the refrigerated container; fortunately, he told them, they would not need to be there long, because the distance from Dover to Des's freight company offices was only a little over twenty miles.

'What must we do when we leave you?' asked Ana Maria anxiously.

'I will drop you before I drive into our lorry compound,' Des replied, 'and when I have finished all the paperwork, I will get in my car and come and take you to the railway station, where you will be able to catch a train to London.'

'We have no money,' said Marius. 'So how will we buy tickets?'

'I will give you enough money for the tickets,' Des reassured him.

'You are very kind,' said Ana Maria. 'Thank you!'

Des closed the back doors of the container, then seated himself once more in the driving-seat, all fingers firmly crossed, for he was well aware of the risk he was taking. As the lorries started to roll off the ferry he continued to think about his illegal passengers, and said to himself, 'It may be against the law, but if it is, the law is an ass. How could anybody know two such nice young people as Ana Maria and Marius and not see they are ordinary, genuine, loving parents, and with such delightful kids too! How can little children like that be classed as criminals? I don't care if I have broken the law – it would be cruel to have done nothing!'

As he drove off the ferry, Des showed his passport as required, along with the various shipping and customs documents, and breathed a silent sigh of relief as he was waved through, and began the final leg of his trip. A few miles short of his home depot he pulled into a lay-by where a number of other long-distance trucks were also parked. He immediately went to the back of his truck, opened the rear doors and let out his passengers, then drove off again, assuring Marius and Ana Maria that he would be returning in his own car to take them to the station in not more than an hour's time.

Not more than ten minutes later, a police car swung into the lay-by and pulled up a few feet from where Marius and his family were sitting waiting for Des's return. Two police officers alighted, approached them and asked to see their papers. Since they had none, and since the two policemen did not possess even Des's linguistic skills, the Romanian family were ordered to get into the police car, and taken back to the immigration offices at Dover for interrogation, which was carried out with the help of a Romanian interpreter.

In the meantime, Des had returned to the lorry depot, had checked in and had a little chat with one or two of the transport firm's employees, then, his working day over, went as quickly as he could to pick up his car and drive back to the lay-by where he had dropped off his illegal passengers. When he got there, however, he found no trace of them. He looked high and low, but there was still no sign of them. He went into the café to look for them, then out again to the car park, and eventually had to conclude that they must have decided to make their own way. Perhaps there had been a misunderstanding, a breakdown in communication, which, after all, would have been eminently possible. At last he gave up searching for them, returned to his car and drove home, where he knew that Thelma would be waiting for him with a meal ready to be be put on the table, as there always was.

Even so, Des was extremely worried about his new acquaintances. His preliminary thoughts concerned how much they would have been delighted with the meal Thelma had prepared, but gradually they turned to a worry that they might have been picked up by the police and interrogated, and possibly deported right away. Of course Des believed in his heart of hearts, as many British people do, that the British police would act responsibly and respectfully, and would not subject them to the sort of treatment that they might have met if they had been arrested by the French police, the Russian police, or the Egyptian police, or any other police force in the world. Of course he was well aware, as everyone is, that on occasions even the British police mistreat their captives; but surely their hearts would melt, just as his had melted after he had been speaking to Marius and Ana Maria for just a matter of minutes. But still he worried...

In fact, unbeknown to Des, the policemen who actually took the Romanian family into custody did treat them with respect and courtesy, allowing them to consult a lawyer, while, at the same time, letting them know that, although the family would not be split up, the most likely outcome for the whole family would still be deportation.

The lawyer who came to see them was a young man who, obviously, had not met them before, so Marius made a point of stressing to him that he too was a lawyer. This turned out to be a crucial factor, for, when the family finally appeared before a magistrate, their counsel said to him that, in speaking to Marius, he had learned that the latter was as able a lawyer as he was, and the magistrate took the unusual step of allowing him to conduct his own defence.

Marius grasped this opportunity with both hands, and told the court at length about the brutality of the Romanian regime at that time, how outspoken he himself had been, and what sort of treatment would be meted out to him by the *Securitate* if he were to be deported and forcibly repatriated.

As a result, admittedly after a number of seemingly endless hearings, Marius and his family were allowed to stay in Britain for six months, a period which might be extended, if they all proved amenable and well behaved.

Naturally Des knew nothing about this, and he worried endlessly about what might have befallen them: had they been deported to Romania? Were they in prison, even the children? Were they even still alive?

In the meantime Des was still driving, undertaking on average two continental trips a week, and every time he was seated in that cab, he thought about Marius, Ana Maria, and their little children.

Apart from wondering what had become of the Romanian family, Des hardly thought about what had happened; in particular, he was extremely relieved that there had apparently been no come-back, for at the back of his mind – and on occasions at the front of his mind – he had envisaged the possibility of a visit by the police, which might even have led to his dismissal from the haulage firm.

A couple of weeks after he had first met the young Romanians, he was driving back from yet another journey to Barcelona, with yet another load of Spanish tomatoes, and drove off the ferry at Dover, just as he had done a few weeks earlier; this time, however, he had no illegal passengers to worry about. He drove up to the passport control, and handed his passport to the official, who was quite young, and whom Des had not met before, but instead of the normal five-second formality, he was kept waiting for several minutes while the official examined his passport and checked some papers.

'Would you mind driving over into that lay-by?' the official asked. 'We need to have a further word.'

'Why?' asked Des. 'What's the problem?'

'Just do as I say,' the official instructed him curtly. 'We need to have a look inside your truck.'

'I don't understand,' said Des. 'You don't normally bother.'

'Just drive over there,' the official repeated.

So Des did as he was told, thinking that this was just for show; the young official probably had a new supervisor, who, in a fit of keenness in the early days of a new job, was trying to make a mark with his new team.

But then a dozen men descended on the truck, and searched it from top to bottom. 'What are you looking for?' Des asked, but he received no answer.

After the search proved fruitless, the senior officer approached Des.

'Mr Wilson,' he began. 'You don't have any passengers today then?'

'No,' he replied. 'I don't carry passengers, I just carry freight.'

'Except when you don't.'

'The only times I don't carry freight are when I don't have a load on the return trip,' he said, 'but that's not likely to happen at this time of year.'

'I'm not talking about carrying freight. I'm talking about carrying passengers.'

'I don't carry passengers.'

'That's not what I've heard.'

'Then you've heard wrong,' said Des.

'Have I now! Do you never carry passengers then?'

'No, never.'

'I'll ask again. Have you ever brought any passengers across the Channel on your lorry?'

'No, never!'

'Never?'

'Never.'

'And you never pick up hitchhikers?'

'I have done. But only when I'm on a long journey and I feel like having a bit of company.'

'Like a couple of weeks ago, you mean?'

'I don't know what you're driving at...'

'A young Romanian couple, with two or three kids, for instance?'

'Oh, you mean Marius and Ana-Maria!'

The official's eyes lit up. 'Ah! You remember them then? Was she nice-looking, Ana Maria?'

'I don't know. I didn't think of her in that way. Yes, I suppose she was. What's that got to do with anything?'

The official ignored Des's question and continued, 'How much did they pay you to bring them over from France?'

'Nothing.'

'Ah, you do admit that you brought them over from France?'

'I might have done...'

'For nothing? You don't expect me to believe that, do you?'

'They were a nice young family, a respectable family. He is a lawyer...'

'And I suppose he sweet-talked himself into your lorry, did he?'

'No, it wasn't like that!'

'What was it like then?'

'They had had a rough time in Romania, and they had nothing, and they were nice people, very nice people, and they had absolutely nothing. I just felt sorry for them.'

'You felt sorry enough to make you break the law?'

'I didn't break the law.'

'Bringing illegal immigrants into Britain is a crime!'

'I didn't know they were illegal immigrants.'

'Did they have passports?'

'I don't know. It's not my job to check passports.'

'No, it's my job, and that of the men who work for me. So, when you drove through Passport Control, where were they? In the cab?'

'No, they were in the truck, in the back.'

'And why didn't you put them in the cab?'

Des made no answer.

'Because you knew they needed to hide when they went through Passport Control, didn't you?'

'Oh, all right, I suppose I did. But they were just decent, ordinary people, and I felt sorry for them. And I'd do the same tomorrow.'

'Oh, would you now? I think I've heard enough. You can tell your story to the police now.'

'The police?'

'Yes, the police. The people whose job it is to keep our country safe from every Tom, Dick and Harry that wants to come here!'

With that, the official summoned a police officer who led Des away, and Des spent the next few hours being subjected to a further interrogation by the police, who eventually let him go, by which time it was nearly midnight, and Des slept in his cab in a lay-by just outside Dover.

At about two o'clock in the morning Des was awoken by the sound of his mobile ringing. He fumbled for it in his pocket, drew it out, noticed that the call was from a number with which he was unfamiliar, but he answered the call anyway.

'Hello?' he said.

'Are you listening?' said a woman's voice, which again he did not recognise.

'Yes,' he replied, completely puzzled.

'This is very important. I did not call the police. It was your family that called the police.'

'I don't understand. What do you mean?'

But the caller had rung off.

The following morning Des drove the rest of the journey to Canterbury, parked his lorry and went into the office.

'Oh, Des,' said one of the secretaries who worked there, 'Mr Jarvis wants to see you.'

'Oh, okay,' said Des. 'I just want to give my wife a ring first. Is it anything important?'

'He said he wants to see you straight away,' said the secretary, so Des went straight in to see the General Manager, without phoning Thelma.

Ten minutes later Des emerged from the General Manager's office; he no longer had a job. He had been fired.

When Des arrived home Thelma was waiting for him at the door. 'You're late,' she said, 'I was expecting you last night. Did you have a puncture or something?'

'No. It was red tape at Dover.'

Thelma looked at her husband. 'Have you been crying?' she asked.

'No, I don't think so,' he replied, not very convincingly, rubbing his eyes with a handkerchief.

'You have!' Thelma said, almost triumphantly. 'What's the matter? Have you had an accident?' Her mind had suddenly switched back twenty or thirty years, when Des had accidentally killed a little boy because he did not know that the boy had been playing at the rear of the vehicle; it was the last time Thelma had seen Des's eyes full of tears.

'No, not an accident,' he said. 'I've got the sack!'

'The sack? They can't give you the sack! You've been there over thirty years!'

'It makes no difference how long you've been there! If you break the law, that's it!'

'Break the law? You've never broken the law!'

'I have now! Or they think I have, which comes to the same thing...'

'Are you going to fight it?'

'No, there's no point.' And he went on to tell her about the police interrogation.

'And this is all because you took pity on that poor Romanian family you told me about?'

'That's right.'

'Well, I would have done the same, and I didn't even meet them!'

'So you'd have been out of a job too!' he said. 'A pretty mess we'd have been in then with both of us out of work! I'm sorry, love!' And he burst into tears again.

'Sorry? What about?' was her answer. 'I'm very proud of you actually, taking pity on that little family! How can they punish little children like that! They didn't ask to be born in a nasty country!'

'I know,' said Des, 'but what am I going to do now? I'll never get another job!'

'We'll manage,' said Thelma. 'I rather like being married to a man who has principles, especially if he puts them into practice!'

Three or four days previously, just after Des had set off on the outward leg of what was to become his final journey at the wheel of a big lorry, Sally, one of the secretaries in the haulage firm's offices, had telephoned the police.

In fact she had spent just over two weeks mulling over whether to act upon the information she had been given: she had discovered that Des had given a lift to some illegal immigrants, her informant having been one of the other drivers.

Sally had not been working for the firm for many months, but her boyfriend was something of a political animal, and was possessed of some extreme right-wing views, as was the driver who had informed her of Des's transgression. She did not know Des very well, but, when she learnt that he had had some Romanians in his lorry, she had discussed it with her boyfriend, who eventually persuaded her that he was a danger to British society, and therefore deserved to be taught a lesson.

After she had made her phone call to the police, however, she had been stricken with a little remorse, but not enough for her to recant and withdraw her accusation. That evening she had been talking in the pub to a friend named Lilian, and told her that she had been the cause of Des's dismissal.

'What are you going to about it then?' said her friend.

'I don't know, Lil,' she replied. 'I don't want anybody to know that I've snitched on him, even if he has done wrong.'

'How would anybody know?'

'I'm afraid that the driver will guess that it was me, because I'm the Manager's secretary...'

'And what if he did?'

'I wouldn't want anybody to think badly of me, Lil. I was just thinking... Would you do something for me?'

'It depends what it is.'

'I thought if you telephoned him...'

'Who?'

'The driver. And I thought if you pretended to be me...'

'But I don't even work at your place.'

'So much the better!'

'And my voice doesn't sound anything like yours...'

'That doesn't matter. There's no need to say who's calling. It's just a matter of making it clear that whoever called the police it wasn't somebody from work, it was... oh, I don't know, somebody from his own family...'

The conversation continued for several minutes, and eventually a form of words had been formulated, and Lil had agreed to make the call to Des that night.

It was not until after Des had broken the news to Thelma that he been dismissed from his job that he also related to her the story of the phone call he had received in the lay-by at dead of night, although it had been preying on his mind for some considerable time, particularly the part of the message which specified that it was a member of his family who had called the police, for that could only have been Thelma. Des and Thelma had no children, neither of them had brothers or sisters, and it was quite a long time since their parents had died; nor had either of them had any uncles, aunts or cousins, a lack which Des had often regretted in the past, especially at Christmas and on special occasions such as birthdays.

When Des did mention it to his wife, Thelma denied vehemently that she had been in touch with the police herself, a denial which Des accepted readily, for he himself considered the likelihood of her shopping him to the police as a possibility so remote that it was not even worth thinking about.

'One of the things I find difficult to fathom,' said Thelma when she heard about it, 'is why anyone should have made that call at all. Why should anybody have been so keen to deny that they had called the police themselves, particularly when they were equally eager to maintain their anonymity? I think it's probably someone who has a guilty conscience about it...'

'I suppose that's quite possible,' said Des, 'but I can't think who it could have been.'

'It's all very strange, isn't it?' said Thelma. 'I wonder if whoever it was who called the police was afraid that you might recognise her voice. Who is there at work who might have been in a position to find out what you did, or to overhear gossip about it?'

'I have to say, the voice I heard on the phone didn't sound like anyone I know, and I've known most people at work for years, so it couldn't possibly have been somebody from work! And then there aren't many women in the place at all. The only ones I can think of are two or three secretaries in the office. I suppose if one of the drivers had come in at the end of a trip blabbing about what he'd seen or what he'd been told, one of those secretaries might have been in a position to hear what was said.'

'Would any of the drivers have talked about something like that?'

'Yes, there are one or two who shoot their mouth off now and again about there being too many foreigners in Britain these days – usually the people who are least likely to have come across any!'

'Were there any other people from your firm likely to have been in Dover at the time you were?'

'I don't know, let me think...'

'Don't think about your last trip then, think about the trip when you picked up the Romanians...'

'Ah, yes, I seem to remember there was one who drove past when I was dropping off Marius, Ana Maria and the kids at the lay-by just down the A2 from the office...'

'What was his name?'

'I can't think... He's a nasty piece of work, I don't like him very much... Gerry, I think his name is... Gerry... Gerry Sandwell, that's his name! And he's a bit of a fascist, not likely to be a friend of anybody wanting to come into our country, even legitimately!'

'But if it was Gerry Sandwell, what can you do about it now?'

'Not a lot, to be honest! I suppose I might go over to the truck yard, seek him out and knock his block off...'

'Would that solve anything?'

'Not really, no.'

Almost a year later, Des and Thelma were out shopping together in the centre of Canterbury. Des was still out of work, and, to his surprise, he had heard nothing more from the police about the charge they had warned him he was likely to face. The two of them were just about to come out of Marks and Spencer's, when walking towards them Des saw a smartly dressed young man whose face seemed familiar.

Despite the familiarity of his appearance, Des was astonished when the young man uttered his name. 'Des?' he said. 'Are you Des?'

'Yes, I am,' he answered, 'but I'm sorry, I don't know who you are...'

'Marius,' the young man said, 'I am Marius, from Bucharest...'

'Marius!' Des exclaimed, his face wreathed in smiles, 'What the hell are you doing here?'

'I'm just visiting,' said Marius. 'We live in London these days. This is my first time in Canterbury since I arrived in this country.'

'But look at you! You are so smartly dressed! And you are speaking English! What happened? And why couldn't I find you when I went back to pick you up when I'd just dropped you in Canterbury?'

'The police came back before you did,' Marius explained, and we were taken into custody...'

'Oh dear, that sounds bad!'

'No, it turned out okay in the end,' Marius replied.

'It's so good to see you,' said Des. 'But I'm sorry, you don't know my wife! This is Thelma...'

'It is so good to meet you,' said Marius.

'And how is Ana Maria, and all those lovely children?' said Des.

'They are very well, thanks to you, and the children are growing too.'

'Look,' said Des, 'let's go in this pub and you can tell me your story.'

'All right,' said Marius, 'I've got an hour to spare before my appointment. But I'd better not have too much to drink!'

'Why?'

'Because my next appointment is at Canterbury County Court, and I think the judge might not be impressed if I arrived smelling of drink!'

'Oh, I see,' said Des. 'I suppose you're up on a charge of travelling without a passport or something, are you?'

Marius laughed out loud. 'Nothing like that,' he said, 'I never faced that charge or anything like it! Have you forgotten I'm a lawyer? I'm representing a young man who's applying for political asylum.'

Des, Thelma and Marius went into the pub and Des ordered some sandwiches and a round of drinks – including a glass of lemonade for Marius. During the next half-hour Des learnt how Marius, Ana Maria and the children had been granted political asylum, and how he was now working once more as a lawyer. The family were living comfortably in London – and Marius produced some snaps of his children to prove it.

'What lovely children you have, Marius,' said Thelma. You must come down and see us.'

'We'd love to,' replied Marius. 'After all, we owe everything to your husband. If he hadn't been so kind to us I really think we would all have died! He's a wonderful man!'

'I think so too,' Thelma replied. 'But I think there is perhaps something you could do for him in return...'

'I would be happy to,' said Marius. 'What is it?'

'Although Des is very happy today, because he's found you again, he's not been at all happy recently, because he lost his job.'

'Lost his job?'

'Yes, because he helped you and your family, he was dismissed from his job, and at his age he can't find another.'

'Why did you lose your job, Des?'

'Because I was accused of transporting illegal immigrants.'

'Were you ever charged?'

'No, I wasn't. The police told me they would charge me, but they never did.'

'So your dismissal was also illegal!'

'Was it?'

'Oh yes. The police obviously did not bring any charge because we were granted political asylum, and therefore you did not do anything illegal, so it was illegal to fire you! Easy! I'll make sure you get your job back! It's the least I can do!'

Within a month Des was reinstated in his job, and remained in it until he eventually retired at the age of sixty. Even more importantly, as far as Des was concerned, Ana Maria, Marius and their children became Des and Thelma's firmest friends, and they saw each other very regularly.

'Maybe you don't go to church regularly,' said Marius one day when they were together, 'but I don't know anyone in the world that puts Christian principles into practice as well as you do!'

'Hear, hear!' said Ana Maria.

As usual, David printed off his latest story and handed it to Margaret, who read it straight away, as she normally did, unless she was busy cooking, or involved with any other project which could not be conveniently abandoned for the time it would take to read David's latest offering.

'What do you think?' asked David when she finally put the last page down. 'Is it up to the standard of the others?'

'Oh yes, it certainly is – in fact it gripped me emotionally as soon as those little children came on the scene. There is only one thing that I was wondering about...'

'And what's that?'

'It was all sorted out pretty quickly, wasn't it? Would it really happen as quickly as that in real life? I mean, political asylum cases can run on for years, can't they?'

'Yes, they can, but that doesn't mean they have to, or even that they necessarily will. I'm sure that all it needs is for one of the crucial players – the judge, for instance – to be keen on it being sorted straight away, especially if there are children concerned. In this case, I grant you, they were very lucky having the judge they did! But somebody has to! So why not one of my characters, particularly if he has right on his side?'

Chapter Five

David set himself to work once more the following Monday morning, although when Margaret asked him, as she usually did, whether he had any plans for his next story, he said he had absolutely no ideas at all.

'I've heard that before! In fact I'm sure that you said exactly the same thing this time last week! So what are you going to do?' she asked.

'I'm going to write,' replied David.

'But what are you going to write?'

'I don't know.'

'How can you write without knowing what you're going to write?'

'I don't know, but something will come.'

'Are you sure?'

'Oh yes.'

'How can you be so sure?'

'Because I've quite often been in this position already, and it always works.'

'But what about your first sentence? You've got to start somehow! How do you know what to put in your first sentence?'

'I don't know. But it doesn't really matter what I write, as long as I get started. I may finish up chucking out the first sentence I've written, or the first paragraph – or even the first page! But my brain usually clicks into action before I reach that point!'

So David began writing, and, just as he had predicted, his brain started to produce coherent thoughts, and he did not even have to discard the first sentence! Here is what he wrote:

John and Muriel Alcock lived in a sizeable detached house in West Bridgford, a well-heeled suburb of the city of Nottingham. Although the inhabitants of West Bridgford regarded themselves as totally independent of the city, they were not reluctant to profit from the city's amenities, which were many, as one would expect of a city whose population, if one included the suburban districts, came close to half a million. Those who lived in West Bridgford also tended to call it simply Bridgford, because, although there was an East Bridgeford in existence, it was much smaller, and some miles away, and, for some reason long forgotten, the names of the places were traditionally spelt differently, although the modern cavalier attitude to spelling has led to many people writing the two names in the same way, although the two places are so different that it would have been impossible for anyone to mistake one for the other. The Alcocks' house was in Wilford Lane, not too far from the world-famous Trent Bridge cricket ground.

'Hey, Carolyn!' John and Muriel's teenage son said to his sister one day. 'I was thinking of asking Mum and Dad if they would let me have a party for my 17th birthday next month. Do you think they'd say yes?'

'You're feeling brave! I shouldn't think they will say yes, not in a million years!' replied Carolyn. 'After all, they don't usually go along with any of our ideas, do they!'

'No, you're right, they don't! But I really would like to have a party, so I think I'm going to give it a go and see what happens. After all, if you don't ask, you don't get!'

'I'll try and be out of the house when you ask them then! I always get the backlash when you upset them!'

Her brother contradicted her, as he usually did, but she had made her escape just in time to avoid hearing his words, because, as a result of long experience, she knew she wouldn't enjoy hearing the comment which was sure to come!

Carolyn and her brother Keith were not exactly the best of buddies, although they did combine effectively when engaged in a battle against their parents, and there were many such battles during their teenage years. In fact it would be no exaggeration to say that no member of the Alcock family was routinely on good terms with the rest of the family. The children – who stubbornly objected to being treated as children – were currently at the most rebellious stage of adolescence, although, it must be admitted, at no period of their life so far could either of them have been described as amenable.

The parents neither understood nor cared very much for their children, or indeed each other, for they had gradually grown apart since their marriage about eighteen years previously, and they had virtually no interests in common; in fact it would have been difficult for anyone to list their interests, for, outside grumbling about each other, the kids, the weather, the cost of living, the council, the government, and pretty well anything else they could find to complain about, there were basically none. Nor did the family eat together on any regular basis: whereas other parents might have insisted on family meals being social occasions which might lead to greater family unity, they had never seemed to accept that as a worthwhile goal.

That evening, when Carolyn was busy doing her homework, Keith took it into his head to tackle his father on the matter of his having a birthday party. 'Dad,' he said, I was wondering if I might have a few friends in for my birthday – you know, a bit of a party...'

'When's your birthday?'

Keith, unusually for him, resisted the temptation to pass some caustic comment to the effect that it was shameful that his father was not even aware of the date of his son's birthday, and restricted himself to a factual answer: 'June the eleventh'.

'Oh, that's a long way away yet! Ask me again nearer the time!'

'How near?'

'Oh, don't bother me now, I'm busy!'

As far as Keith could see, all that his Dad was busy doing was looking at the newspaper, which to Keith did not seem to be a sufficient excuse for giving him the brush-off. So he decided to try his mother. He went into the kitchen where she was emptying the dishwasher. 'Mum,' he said, 'I was wondering if I might have a party on my birthday this year?'

'You'll have to ask your dad.'

'I just did.'

'And what did he say?'

'He said ask me another time, I'm busy.'

'What's he busy doing then?'

'He's reading the paper.'

'Is that all? Then go and ask him again.'

'Well, what do you think?'

'I don't know. I'm busy.'

As far as Keith was concerned, being busy emptying the dishwasher was no more of a reason for dismissing his question than his dad's being busy reading the newspaper, so he asked again.

'Mum, you're only emptying the dishwasher – answer me!'

'What do you want to know?' said his mother, who had not really been listening the first time he had asked.

'I want to know if I can have a party on my 17th birthday?'

'You'll have to ask your father.'

'He's busy.'

'I thought you said he was only reading the paper... Go and ask him again.'

So Keith went in to see his father again, but this time he decided to change his approach.

'Dad,' he said, 'I've just asked Mum if I can have a party on my 17th birthday.'

'And what did your mother say?'

'She said it was all right with her if it was all right with you...'

'Did she now? Oh well, I suppose I'd better go along with what your mother says... Anything for a quiet life!'

This was the answer Keith was hoping for. Admittedly there was still a possibility that his father might discover that he had been tricked into an affirmative response, but the fireworks which might ensue when it eventually struck him could be dealt with when they actually started exploding, he thought.

So he immediately went back into the kitchen and told his mother that his dad had said yes, he could have a party.

'Did he?' she remarked, an element of surprise being conveyed by her tone.

'Yes, I was a bit surprised too,' said Keith, who then beat a retreat so as to avoid any interrogation his mother might choose to embark upon. As he was returning to his room, Carolyn was coming out of hers, her homework complete – or as much of it as she felt like completing, for she never took homework really seriously – so Keith told his sister the good news.

'Oh, I'm very surprised,' she said. 'I suppose neither of them said anything about me inviting some of my friends too, did they?'

'No,' replied Keith, giving the shortest possible answer, for he hated the very idea of his little sister – who was barely a year younger than him – rustling in on his 'grown-up' birthday party!

'Huh!' was Carolyn's instant comment, and she went off to the kitchen to tackle her mother.

'Mum,' she said, 'I understand that Keith's going to have a party for his birthday...'

'Yes?' said her mother, sensing that a question was following not too far behind.

'Well, I was thinking, Keith's friends are all a lot older than mine, and they won't want to be bothered with a lot of silly little girls, as I'm sure they call us...'

'I'm sure they wouldn't...'

'I've heard some of them say exactly that! Anyway, there's an easy answer. If I can invite half a dozen of my best friends and we keep out of the way, I'm sure that will do the trick...'

Then Carolyn left the kitchen. This was an effective technique she had recently developed which always resulted in her having the last word herself, as well as assuring herself of a quiet period during which she could prepare her next gambit: she would raise a contentious question, immediately propose what she claimed to be an easy solution, then leave the room before the person to whom she was speaking had time to reply.

The next time her father set eyes on Carolyn, however, he reopened the discussion. 'I understand that your mum has agreed that you can invite some of your friends to Keith's birthday party...'

'Yes,' she said, anticipating that some sort of restriction was about to be imposed.

'Then I think, if you do, we ought to limit the number of people you invite to five,' he said.

'Oh, Dad! That's no good!'

'Why not?'

'Because I've got more than five special friends, and if I don't invite all of them, the ones who are left out will never talk to me again!'

'In that case, they're not very special friends, are they!'

'Oh Dad! It's all very well for you to mock, but I'm the one who's going to have to take all the flak!'

Her father had his response prepared. 'So tell me who are your special friends then.'

Carolyn had her own answer ready. 'There's Susan, Megan, Kathleen, Maureen, Joan and Janet for a start... I couldn't possibly leave any of them out!'

Carolyn's father was correct in imagining that all his daughter was doing was simply reciting a list of girls from her class, including some who were not special friends at all. But she hadn't yet finished, and she continued: 'And then there's Joyce, Patricia, Kathleen...'

'You've already counted Kathleen...' her father objected.

'There's Kathleen McNeill and Kathleen Connor,' she continued. 'You see, there are two Kathleens!'

'I make that nine so far anyway!'

'I haven't finished yet, Dad!'

'I have though! I said you could invite five of your friends. If you go on at that rate you'll be inviting even more than your brother will...'

'So what!' she retorted, tossing her head in a way she knew very well her father found extremely irritating, and leaving the room abruptly. Since Carolyn usually managed to get her own way by simply ignoring the controversial topic until her parents had forgotten that there had been some controversy, she simply said nothing about it for several weeks, then sent out the invitations without saying anything to anyone: no more was said, therefore, of her guests being limited to five in number.

Other discussions, however, continued to take place about Keith's party – at irregular intervals – for several weeks, mostly between Carolyn and either her father or mother – and sometimes both, to such an extent that

Keith began to feel as if it was not going to be his party at all, because his sister appeared to have hijacked it.

Such discussions generally arose out of the imposition of prohibitions – Carolyn had been strictly warned that there was to be no smoking and no alcohol for any of the girls, although when she raised the objection that most of the boys would be smoking and drinking, her father exploded: 'Not if I see them, they won't!'

This, of course, led in turn to an altercation between Keith and his father, Keith arguing that at a party held at Christmas in the house of one of his friends, the parents themselves had been handing out cigarettes and pouring drinks for the boys. John's riposte was to the effect that that sort of thing might very well have happened at somebody else's house, but it would never be allowed in theirs. No mention was made of drugs, however, either because John and Muriel were totally ignorant of the recent popularity of drug-taking among young people, or else because they would never have imagined that their children – or any acquaintances of their children – could possibly stoop so low.

The other bone of contention concerned music. Disagreement on this topic first reared its head in an argument between Keith and Carolyn – although their parents had to have their say too. First of all came the question of what sort of music would be played, which seemed to amount to a tendency among the girls to prefer country and western or blues, and among the boys to prefer heavy metal and punk. As far as John and Muriel were concerned, it was simply a choice between Keith's cacophony and Carolyn's cacophony: one was as bad as the other, and the parents perceived no difference.

Then there was the question of the nature of the lyrics; Muriel had read somewhere that the BBC had recently banned a particular song from the airwaves because of the unsuitability of its lyrics. If challenged, she could not have named the song or the singer, and she had never heard it either, but she was adamant that no such music would ever be heard in her house. Her argument carried no weight with her husband, however: his line was that all pop song lyrics were incomprehensible anyway, so it didn't matter what words the singer was mouthing, because nobody would understand it unless they could lip-read, which of course would be literally impossible for anyone just listening on an audio system.

Then there was the question of volume. Both parents preferred the music to be quiet enough for conversation to be audible in the same room, although it was many years since they had themselves murmured sweet nothings to each other while dancing; both children accepted as axiomatic that no one would want to hold a conversation when one was dancing anyway.

The matter of timing also caused a measure of disagreement. John considered the party should have ended altogether by 10.30 pm, whilst Muriel was willing to extend the closing-time until midnight, although she thought the music should have ceased by 11.

Then there was turmoil when Keith and Carolyn suddenly mentioned the possibility of some guests staying overnight; both parents would only accept the idea if those staying were either all male or all female; naturally, John wanted to restrict the right to stay overnight to boys only, whilst Muriel wanted only girls to be allowed to stay.

In other words, there was so little consensus on what was acceptable that the whole idea was a recipe for disaster; however, when John went as far as to suggest that the whole project of holding a party be abandoned on those very grounds, both Keith and Carolyn sulked for several days, and made life even more difficult for their parents than it habitually was.

Even the least perspicacious observer would have felt that there was so much evidence that the proposed party was likely to fail that everyone involved should have agreed that the whole thing be scrapped, but in reality there was too much at stake: in such a remarkably dysfunctional family there was so much resentment and so many scores to settle that nobody really wished to lose this opportunity to make their point. So go ahead it did.

On the matter of overnight stays, at length a compromise was agreed, although both John and Muriel felt that it was defeat rather than compromise, and they were probably right: the agreement was that two boys and two girls would be allowed to stay the night, because there were two bedrooms free, one for the girls to share, one for the boys.

There was so little chance of agreement over the matter of who should be invited that both Keith and Carolyn invited as many as they wished; to that extent it was one up to the children, although it was a Pyrrhic victory in that it only came about because the parents had stopped talking about it. Even so, there were a number of gate-crashers, both boys and girls – although the parents had so little control that neither of them would have been able to say who was a gate-crasher and who was not.

Word had spread early about the proposed ban on alcohol and tobacco: as a result there was plenty of both about. Nor was it simply the gate-crashers who were responsible, for the message passed on by both Keith and Carolyn beforehand was in effect: if you want a 'proper' drink at this party, you'll have to bring your own. In consequence, even in the early stages of the party both house and garden were strewn with empty bottles of gin, vodka and tequila, although in truth most of those bottles had been started well before their owners arrived at the party.

In the battle for control of the music, first blood was drawn by Carolyn, for the first record that was played that evening was of Neil Diamond singing *Sweet Caroline*. Her early advantage was soon nullified, however, for before Neil Diamond's song had even finished, Keith made sure it was replaced by a song by the *Sex Pistols*, played at a volume which ensured not only that his parents could not help but hear it, but also that they would understand the obscenities with which it was packed.

Keith's father John then made his first attempt to intervene, but as soon as he came anywhere near the record player, a phalanx of adolescent boys formed to prevent his switching the music off; John immediately withdrew, intimidated by the aggression and the bad language of the young men.

Muriel also made her views known, although her approach was more subtle: she drew Carolyn to one side and told her, 'If you and Keith want this party to continue, you must inform your guests that the music must be much less loud, with no obscenities, and we will not tolerate any violence or aggressive behaviour.'

Carolyn's response was a helpless 'What do you think I can do about it? I don't like this music any more than you do!'

Her mother retorted calmly, 'Just let your brother know that if the music is not quieter and more acceptable to us within the next few minutes, your Dad will switch off the record player at the mains and send everybody home. This is our home after all, and we are not willing to accept this level of noise, and the neighbours certainly won't!'

Carolyn passed on her mother's warning to her brother, but his reaction was simply, 'It's out of my hands. I can't do anything about it on my own. It's the fault of the gate-crashers. They are the only ones who are being aggressive. Plus one or two of your girlfriends, of course – I told Mum and Dad there'd be trouble if you invited any of your friends!' Carolyn was furious, which had of course been Keith's intention, but her fury was such that she did not convey Keith's reaction to her mother, which had also been Keith's objective.

John, however, had decided that it was time that he reacted himself, because, although a quarter of an hour had passed since his ultimatum had been delivered to his son, the *Sex Pistols* were still screaming out their crudities from the loudspeakers. Keith was therefore extremely surprised when he saw his father approaching him wielding a pair of large garden shears. 'What are you going to do with those, Dad?' he said. 'You must be mad! Take those away!'

'Not until you've switched that hideous row off!' he yelled. 'And if you don't, I'm going to cut the lead to that record player with these! And if I cut the lead, you won't be able to plug it in anywhere!'

Keith swore at his father, which made John see red, and, just at that moment, the front doorbell rang. John immediately went to see who was at the door, and found it was their next door neighbours complaining about the noise, at which he became even more furious, for they appeared to believe that the noise was his responsibility. His reaction was to go and confront his son again, and drag him to the door, saying to the neighbours, 'This is the person in charge of the music, not me! Speak to him!'

To his dismay, and to that of the neighbours too, his son then emitted a torrent of invective which would have made even the likes of Sid Vicious and Johnny Rotten blush, after which he slammed the door in the face of the neighbours.

'Right,' said his father, 'I'm going to cut that lead!' But, before he could even get close to the record player, a mob of young men jumped on him and wrested the shears from his grasp, and at that moment the doorbell rang again.

Seeing that her husband was currently in no position to answer the door, Muriel went to open it, assuming that it was the next door neighbours again. But it was not: this time it was the police.

'Are you in charge here?' demanded one of the policemen.

'If only!' she replied.

'You either are or you aren't,' said the other policeman. 'We've had a lot of complaints about the noise coming from your party.'

'It's not my party!'

'Then whose is it?'

'It's my son's party, and I only wish I did have some control! But there are a lot of gatecrashers, and they've been making it difficult for anybody to restore order. Come on in, and you can speak to them. If they'll listen to you, that's more than they'll do for us!'

Muriel then led the two policemen into the lounge, where Keith was standing by the record player; as soon as Keith caught sight of the police officers he immediately reduced the volume of the music, at which there was an immediate uproar of protest. Seeing themselves surrounded by aggressive teenagers, the policemen decided to call for reinforcements, and went back to the front door. Two minutes later they were back, with another four policemen in tow. This time they approached John.

'Are you the householder?' they asked.

'Yes, I am, but I'm not responsible for this chaos!' John declared.

'Would you be happy for us to take charge then, seeing that you're not in control?'

'Yes, whatever you say! I've tried, but they won't listen to me!'

One of the policemen then approached a young man standing by the record player and nonchalantly smoking a cigarette, without realising that the young man was actually the son of the householder. 'Would you mind if I have a look at that cigarette you're smoking, sir?' the policemen said, in a way that made it abundantly clear that Keith really had no choice in the matter.

'Yes, okay,' said Keith, handing the cigarette to the officer, who immediately smelt it, and called the police sergeant over.

'Look, sarge, I reckon this is hash, what do you think?'

The police sergeant sniffed, and agreed. 'Yes, I think you're right.' Then, addressing Keith he went on,

'I'm charging you with being in possession of a Class B drug.'

Hearing this, John went berserk. 'You can't do that!' he shouted. 'That's my son!'

'If that's your son,' the police sergeant said, 'you should exercise more control.'

'How dare you? You can't come into somebody's house like that and start throwing your weight about!'

'I was under the impression that you invited me to,' said the sergeant, 'in which case I can do as I please, including charging you for allowing your home to be used for the misuse of drugs and obstructing the police in the performance of their duty.'

John was furious, but remained silent, and was even more incensed when he became aware that Keith was sniggering at what the police sergeant had just said to his father.

But the sergeant hadn't yet finished with Keith. Because John had interrupted him while he was in the process of charging Keith with possession of drugs, he had not completed the statutory statement, and was obliged to start again.

'Are you Keith Alcock?' he began.

'Yes.'

'Keith Alcock, I am charging you with being in possession of a Class B drug. You do not have to say anything, but it may harm your defence if you do not mention when questioned something which you later rely on in court. Anything you do say may be given in evidence.'

'But this is only a herbal cigarette!' Keith protested. 'It's not cannabis or anything like that!'

'Are you sure?' said the police sergeant. 'It smells like cannabis to me!'

'The boy who gave it to me said it was just a herbal cigarette,' said Keith.

'What was the name of the boy who gave it to you?'

'I have no idea. I've never seen him before.'

'But I believe it's your party, isn't it...'

'Yes, but we've got a lot of gatecrashers...'

'Well, you're still charged, but I'll take the cigarette for analysis anyway.'

Keith stubbed out the cigarette and handed it to the police sergeant.

'Now then,' the sergeant said, 'I'm going to need the name and address of everyone here. After that, everyone can go home, the party's over!'

At that announcement there was a hum of discontent among all the partygoers; neither did the junior policemen appear too enthusiastic at the idea of having to take down so many names and addresses, but they all pulled out their notebooks and proceeded to carry out the sergeant's order.

At length the task was done, and the partygoers all went home, except for the handful that had been given permission to spend the night there. Keith and Carolyn, totally deflated by their experience, took themselves to bed, and John and Muriel followed suit; it was 1.30 in the morning.

About three quarters of an hour later, John was awakened by the sound of his bedside telephone ringing. He stretched out his arm and took the handset from its cradle. 'Hello,' he said.

'Are you listening?' asked a female voice which he did not recognise, although afterwards he thought it might have been the voice of one of their next door neighbours who had come earlier to complain about the noise.

'Yes,' said John.

'This is important,' said the voice. 'I did not call the police. It was your family who called the police.'

'What do you mean?' asked John, but the caller had terminated the call.

John went back to bed, but could not help pondering over what the caller had said, and also over the events of the evening. 'I did not call the police,' the caller had said. If John was right in thinking that the person on the phone had been their next door neighbour, that would at least make sense: the neighbours would, after all, have been aware of the arrival of more than one police car, and they were perhaps worried that he would assume that, in addition to going round to complain about the noise earlier, they had gone on to call the police.

But then she had said, 'It was your family that called the police.' He knew that he had not summoned the police himself, and he was pretty sure that neither had his wife. That left only two people who might have called them: his son or his daughter.

The first person John saw on coming downstairs the following morning was his daughter Carolyn. He was about to ask her if it was she who had called the police, but then past experience told him that a direct question such as that would bring an instant denial, regardless of whether or not it was the truth. Consequently he asked, rather more tactfully, he thought, 'Carolyn, have you any idea who actually called the police last night?'

He was prepared for an evasive answer at best, but in fact she answered without hesitation: 'Oh yes, I know who it was. It was Keith.'

'Keith?' John replied. 'But why on earth would Keith do that, especially when he was smoking those dodgy cigarettes himself?'

'He had no idea they were dodgy. I was there when this boy offered him one, and what Keith told the policeman was true.'

'That they were herbal cigarettes, you mean?'

'Yes. I heard him say it.'

'So, even if they were cannabis or something like that, Keith had no idea?'

'No idea at all, no. Keith wouldn't have had one if he hadn't been assured they were okay...'

'Thank God for that... You are telling me the truth, aren't you, Carolyn?'

'Of course I am! When did you last hear me defend my brother?'

'I can't remember.'

'And neither can I! You know as well as I do that I don't really get on with Keith – if he was really at fault I would probably be the one that would have dropped him in it!'

'Oh, I think that's going a bit far...'

'Look, Dad, Keith and I hate each other's guts! We can't stand each other! Never have done, and never will! Full stop! He knows that as well as I do.'

'But why would Keith have called the police to his own party?'

'Ask him yourself! I have no idea, except that he was a bit fed up with you... And me, for that matter, because I made a point of getting to the record player first.'

At that point Keith came downstairs, and John was able to ask him directly. 'Keith, what made you call the police to your own party last night?'

'Who said I did?'

'Oh, come on, Keith, everyone knows you did! You didn't really make a secret of it, did you?' said Carolyn.

'Because I was fed up with the party and I thought it would be a good laugh.'

'And so that you could get your dad into trouble as well,' Carolyn added.

'Well, that too,' Keith admitted shamefacedly. 'I'm sorry, Dad. I was really fed up.'

'About what?'

'Because all we have in this house is rows! Rows between you and Mum, rows between me and Carolyn, rows between one of us kids and Mum or you, it never ends... And I've had enough!'

'So have I, Dad!' Carolyn added.

At that point Muriel also came downstairs, and was made aware that they were all fed up with the hostile atmosphere which pervaded their home. Fortunately Muriel too had enough sense not to resort to her habitual answer to the effect that it was none of her doing; she answered, 'I've had enough too. Last night was the last straw. It was the first time the police have ever been involved in any of our altercations, and I really felt ashamed. I'm sorry if any of it was my fault.'

'And so am I,' said John.

'Me too,' said both Carolyn and Keith.

An hour later a policeman came to the house and informed Keith that no further action would be taken in connection with the offence he had been charged with the previous night, because tests had shown that the confiscated cigarette was harmless, and John suggested they should all go out together for a celebratory lunch.

'What are we celebrating?' Carolyn asked.

'Publicly, I think we'll make it Keith's 17th birthday,' said John. 'But deep inside myself, I think it's more to do with the end of hostilities!'

They all smiled, then went out and enjoyed lunch.

David printed off his story and Margaret read it. As soon as she had finished, she commented, 'We know that Keith called the police himself, but we aren't told who the voice on the telephone was! So who was it?'

'I don't know! Possibly one of the neighbours, possibly one of Keith's friends. Why does it matter?'

'Because the readers want to know!'

'Well, they'll have to use their imagination then! There's nothing wrong with that, is there?'

'No, of course not! That's up to you. But what a dysfunctional family you've invented! Where did you dream that up from?'

'I have no idea! I just created the characters, and they just started reacting to one another.'

'They were a really nasty bunch, weren't they? Did they all live happily ever after? I don't suppose so! I wonder how long that truce will last! What do you think?'

'It depends how fed up they all are with the vicious circle that they got sucked into,' said David. 'I know that writing about it made me thoroughly depressed, so I hope it turns out all right in the end!'

'Well, if you don't know, who on earth does?' was Margaret's final comment.

Chapter Six

Exactly seven days later, Margaret said to David, 'I expect as usual you haven't the remotest idea what you're going to write this week, have you?'

'No, for once you're wrong! I had a wakeful spell during the night, and I started thinking about the book, and lo and behold! an idea came into my head!'

'That's wonderful! Am I allowed to know what it's about?'

'Not quite yet, no. I don't know myself how it's going to turn out, but I know roughly how I'm going to start. Actually I've had something along these lines at the back of my mind for quite a while, but I didn't want to start on it until I had a good idea which way it would be heading.'

'And now you do know where it's heading, do you?'

'More or less. Funnily enough, it's one of the first ideas I had after the phone call that kicked it all off.'

'Really? So what's it going to be about?'

'Well, as soon as something funny happens in Cheltenham, people start wondering if GCHQ has something to do with it, and I've been racking my brains to find out some way I could use that idea, and now I have an idea – well, it's a starting point anyway! I'll let you have a look at it when it's done!'

'I hate to remind you of this, but I was the first to mention GCHQ in connection with that call you received!'

'Did you? I don't remember, I'm sorry! What did you suggest?'

'I didn't actually suggest anything. It was simply that we were talking about the 'number unobtainable' tone that you kept hearing, and I said that phones at GCHQ can make calls, but if you were to try and find out what number was calling, you wouldn't be able to!'

'Oh, so you did, sorry, I'd forgotten that. Anyway, I'd better crack on!'

'Okay, and I shall look forward to reading all about it!'

Peter Watmough and his wife Joan lived alone in Charlton Kings, a leafy suburb of Cheltenham, just along from the beautiful parish church. Joan was Peter's second wife, and Peter was Joan's second husband. They had no children of their own, but they each had offspring from their earlier marriages: Peter had two sons, now in their late twenties, whilst Joan had a daughter named Lucy, of roughly the same age as Peter's elder son, Andrew.

All three children were married, and lived in the Cheltenham area; they had all moved away from Cheltenham to go to university, but whereas the youngest of them, Richard, had returned to Cheltenham to go into teaching, Lucy and Andrew had returned to enter the Civil Service. But at work, Lucy and Andrew did not spend their time filling in forms or merely pen pushing, for each of them had a good degree in modern languages, Andrew in Russian and Lucy in Mandarin, which was a prime reason for their being enlisted into the Civil Service.

If one approaches Cheltenham from Gloucester, driving along the A40, one's attention is seized on the outskirts of the town by what at first sight appears to be a modern sports stadium: locals, however, term it 'the Doughnut', because of its shape, and there can be few inhabitants of Cheltenham who do not know that it houses the Government Communications Headquarters, otherwise known as GCHQ, an important part of the United Kingdom's security service. Essentially a listening post, GCHQ employs many linguists and mathematicians in highly secret jobs as part of which many of them will work in collaboration with the other branches of the Secret Service, MI5 and MI6, and, indeed, with the security services of our European and transatlantic allies too.

In the early years of the 21st century, however, the work of GCHQ has become much less secretive than it used to be in the past; these days, for instance, everybody knows what it is for, although secrecy surrounds its precise function. In the 1960s and 1970s, however, it was not even named GCHQ; people who worked there simply said that they worked for the Foreign Office, and in off-duty conversation among themselves, they habitually referred to it as 'the office'. That was an era, of course, when most people were much more likely to accept that one was simply not allowed to know certain things, because it was essential for national security: it was only in the 21st century that secrecy became an insult to democracy and therefore GCHQ became obliged to defend its operations in lengthy public enquiries. There were few people, however, who believed unquestioningly what the officers of GCHQ said. Nor were there many who believed that, even if the spokesmen for GCHQ were essentially telling the truth, that it was the simple, unadulterated truth – in fact it was often said among GCHQ employees meeting in private, in a deliberate parody of Oscar Wilde's famous quip, that in GCHQ terms the truth is seldom simple, and never unadulterated.

There can be few inhabitants of Cheltenham either, who do not personally know several GCHQ employees, and virtually all of them accept that asking them what they do is a waste of time, because they are all bound by the Official Secrets Act, which means that very few people even bother to ask about their work. Naturally there are some who do ask; by the same token there are probably some GCHQ employees who are a little less discreet than their employers would like, but, on the whole, if something is supposed to be a secret in Cheltenham, it tends to remain a secret. Even so, the writer David Sumner was correct in claiming that if something strange happens in Cheltenham, there is inevitably a widespread suspicion that GCHQ probably had something to with it.

In 2002 the United Kingdom government and the government of the United States, to say nothing of the United Nations Security Council, were much exercised by the matter of whether the state of Iraq, still under the rule of Saddam Hussein, possessed an indeterminate number of weapons of mass destruction, and the television news was full of it too.

It was not a matter which caused Peter Watmough to lose much sleep, however. As a small town solicitor, spending most of his time on the fairly pedestrian task of conveyancing, this was far from being one of his major interests: he was much more preoccupied with the affairs of his local golf club, of which he was currently Captain. How on earth could Peter become embroiled in the Iraq situation? It would perhaps be stretching credulity a little too far to suggest that he was totally ignorant of the location of Iraq, but he never watched the news and always read the newspaper from the back, starting with the sports news. It was therefore unsurprising that he did not even suspect that GCHQ might be involved with a mysterious phone call of which he was the recipient in the early hours of the morning towards the end of December 2002.

It was just after two o'clock in the morning that his telephone rang, and, naturally, he and his wife were fast asleep. Joan continued to sleep while Peter himself answered the telephone, and, indeed, remained asleep during the whole of Peter's conversation with the caller, who, he was convinced, was none other than his stepdaughter Lucy. This was the full extent of their conversation:

'Hello... Who's that?' said Peter.

'Are you listening?' inquired a female voice.

'Yes, Lucy, I am...'

The caller ignored the fact that Peter had called her Lucy, and continued, 'This is very important. I did not call the police. It was your family who called the police.'

'I'm sorry, I don't understand. Would you mind repeating that?'

But answer came there none, for the caller had replaced the receiver.

Although Peter's head was in a whirl, bearing in mind both the incomprehensibility of the message and the fact that he had been awakened at dead of night to receive the call, he did what most people would have done on receiving a live call from a member of his family by whose message he was not only puzzled but also deeply worried, and immediately rang her back; in those days people knew phone numbers by heart, and were less reliant on new-fangled things like instant redial, so he dialled her number himself. But even after his call he was no nearer to understanding what it was all about, for it was Lucy's husband Ian who picked up the phone, and all he could do was tell Peter that Lucy could not possibly have been the person who called him, because she was fast asleep by his side at that very moment.

The principal reason Peter was worried was because of Lucy's use of the expression 'your family' during the call; technically, of course, Lucy was not a member of Peter's family because the only way they were related was because Peter had married Lucy's mother while Lucy was still in her teens, but even so, Peter found himself extremely distressed to hear his stepdaughter drawing a distinction between 'her family' and his. It was for this reason that Peter found himself on the phone again a few hours later, and once more speaking to his son-in-law Ian, who told him that he would not be able to speak to Lucy right away because she had been called into work that morning 'because something had come up'; in consequence it was mid-afternoon before he could even begin to assuage his concerns.

When he did succeed in catching up with Lucy in the middle of the afternoon, all she was able to do was confirm her husband's statement that she could not possibly have made the call herself because she was fast asleep at the time, although she was able to allay Peter's fears somewhat by saying that she would have been extremely unlikely to use the expression 'your family' to Peter, because as far as she was concerned, they were all one family, and she would never dream of making a distinction between 'Joan's family' and

'Peter's family', stressing, without being prompted, that in her mind Peter was her dad, not her step-dad.

That evening, however, Lucy and Ian happened to be entertaining Peter's son Andrew and Andrew's wife Melanie to dinner, and during the course of the evening Lucy brought up the subject of the phone call that Peter had received; on hearing the message that Peter had been given, all professed themselves as mystified as Peter himself had been as to what it could all have been about. But only ten minutes after Andrew had returned home at the end of the evening, Lucy was surprised to receive a short phone call from him, saying that he had something to say to her about the mysterious phone call, but, whatever she did, she must not mention to Ian, or to anybody else, that he had even phoned her about it. Not that he actually said anything about the call that made sense to Lucy, for all he did was arrange to meet her the following day for lunch in the GCHQ staff canteen and say that what he wanted to talk about was 'office-related'.

When Lucy and Andrew eventually met over lunch the following day, Lucy wasted no time in asking her stepbrother the meaning of his phone call and the significance of his swearing her to secrecy.

'There's absolutely nothing sinister at all about it,' he was quick to assure her, 'but there is nobody outside this establishment that I would be able to discuss it with. But, since we have both signed the Official Secrets Act and are subject to its restrictions, and since we're inside the office, there is no reason at all why I should not share this information with you. But I'm sure I don't need to stress how important it is for you not to tell anybody outside the office what I'm about to tell you.'

Lucy assured him that she was all ears, and would not dream of telling anybody outside GCHQ what her brother was about to tell her, so Andrew went on: 'I was chatting to Dad on the phone yesterday, and he did mention the call he'd received, so I know exactly what the message was that he was given, and, as soon as he told me what it was, I was immediately aware that he was not the intended recipient of the call, because there would be no way in which he would be able to understand the coded message that he received.'

'Coded message?' Lucy replied.

'Yes, a coded message,' he confirmed. 'Nor would you understand the code either, by virtue of the fact that we don't work in the same section. As you know, the way this place works is that there are very few people who are allowed to possess all the pieces of the jigsaw. In fact there are times when I wonder whether there is actually anyone who does! But I suppose we have to make a leap of faith and believe that there is someone for whom it all makes sense, otherwise we wouldn't be able to carry on working here!

'The thing is that the message Dad was given contained the expressions "Are you listening?", "This is very important", "my family", "your family" and "the police". Now in my section the words "Are you listening?" followed by "This is very important" are themselves a coded warning that there are other coded expressions coming up. "My family" means the British, or, more specifically GCHQ, "Your family" means the Americans, and "the police" refers to the United Nations Security Council. Of course, if the person speaking was actually American, "my family" would mean the Americans and "Your family" would apply to the nationality of whatever person he was speaking to. Do you get my drift?'

'Oh yes,' replied Lucy. 'I can see that. But that raises another problem, doesn't it? Dad thought the call must have been from me because the person who rang him spoke like me. Therefore she must have had an English accent, and therefore "My family" must mean the British. But the fact that she also used the expression "Your family" when talking to Dad, that would only make sense if Dad was an American, wouldn't it?'

'Exactly! That is what leads me to the conclusion that Dad was not the intended recipient of the call, which is why I need to tell my superiors about the call he received.'

'So in reality,' said Lucy, 'it was supposed to be a message from a British person to an American, giving them the information that somebody had been talking to the Security Council, but it wasn't the Brits, it must have been the Yanks!'

'That's right. Unless, of course, it was a message from somebody with a British accent working for the American government – and there are some! – in which case it means that it was the Brits who had been talking to the Security Council! In any case, the person who received the call was supposed to be able to interpret the coded messages, which Dad certainly wasn't! And if the Security Council were involved, it must have been something very important, which is why I've already passed on to my Line Manager as much as I know, because somebody obviously dialled the wrong number!'

'What did he say?'

'Very little. But he took very careful notes. He was obviously taking it very seriously, which of course is exactly why he made no comment to me! It's all a question of what any individual needs to know, which is what this place is all about!'

'Which I suppose also means that if you ever do get to hear what it was all about...'

'Which is unlikely...'

'Of course... But if you do, you won't be able to tell me about it!'

'Exactly so! In fact I've probably said more to you than I should! I'd love to know what it's all about, but I'm sure I never will! Anyway, I'd better be getting back to my office – see you soon! And thanks for the lovely meal last night too!'

'You're welcome! Bye, Andrew! See you soon!' replied Lucy.

A couple of weeks later, there was a family get-together at Peter and Joan's house, at which Peter spoke at length about the phone call he had received; Lucy and Andrew each found themselves having to bite their tongue to avoid letting on even the fact that they knew that whoever made the call had made a mistake, and had called Peter in error. Then, when a news flash was broadcast in between programmes on the BBC to the effect that the Americans and British had invaded Iraq – in the eyes of many in contravention of Security Council resolutions, although there were reports that the Security Council actually knew of the invasion even before it happened – Lucy and Andrew had to keep mum, and satisfy themselves with exchanging a knowing wink.

So Peter Watmough never did find out the meaning of the call he received, although he stopped worrying about it, because the principal reason for his concern was that Lucy considered her family and his to be separate entities, and she had made it clear to him that nothing was further from the truth.

Margaret read David's latest chapter, and said, 'I really thought that was going to be about us and our family! This couple were both on their second marriage, and all their children were from the first marriages, in pretty well exactly the same configuration as our family!'

'I know!' replied David. 'Put it down to author laziness!'

'Don't be silly! You lazy? You must be joking!'

'Can I have that in writing? Anyway, even if the Watmough's children were exactly the same age as ours, I couldn't simply reproduce every single detail of our family, because of the changes I needed to make. You see, I needed there to be two people working at GCHQ, because otherwise the story wouldn't work: the only way to let the reader know what happened is for there to be conversations between two people who have signed the Official Secrets Act!'

'Do you think that sort of thing happens at GCHQ?'

'I'm sure it does! In fact I would be surprised if it didn't. I'm sure that there are just as many cock-ups at GCHQ as there are in any other organisation!'

'How can you be so sure?'

'Because it is run by human beings, and human beings make mistakes, like misreading phone numbers, for instance! I'm sure it happens all the time.'

'And our National Security depends on people like that?'

'I know! Pathetic, isn't it! But I'd much rather our security were in the hands of fallible human beings than under the control of infallible computers!'

'Even if there is such a thing as an infallible computer...' said Margaret.

'I think there probably isn't such a thing! The danger with infallibility is that a lot of people tend to think they're infallible themselves!'

'True! But let's get back to your book – which explanation of the phone call is your favourite? Which do you find most convincing?'

'I think they're all plausible so far – let's hope the rest of them appear so! But the GCHQ one, even though it's the shortest, and in one way the most simple, but paradoxically also the most far-reaching – and the most difficult to write – is in my opinion the most likely to be the true one!'

'Why do you think that?'

'Because the importance of a little town like Cheltenham surpasses its size, by far, and the people who work at GCHQ are just as likely to misread or mishear things, and if that happens, inevitably ordinary people like us can get caught up in it, even without realising it. But the global consequences could be far more serious!'

'You're frightening me now! Let's talk about something else. What do you fancy for supper this evening?'

Chapter Seven

The following Monday morning, Margaret said to David over breakfast, ‘I suppose you must be getting towards the end of your book now, are you?’

‘I’m not sure,’ replied David. ‘I mean, for one thing I still have to write the final chapter, which I intend to include the real reason for the phone call. For another, I’m going to write another scenario this week, but, of course, I don’t know how long each scenario is going to be until I’ve nearly finished writing it. I suspect I shall still have to write a further two or three scenarios, quite apart from the final chapter!’

‘Oh,’ said Margaret, ‘I was thinking you must be in the closing stages by now! You seem to have been working on it for so long!’

‘I know!’ said David, ‘It seems a bit like that to me as well!’

'I'm a bit surprised that you don't know how long each scenario is going to be! I assumed that you would have a target length.'

'I did start off with the idea that all the scenarios would be roughly the same length, but I soon abandoned that! It's not actually as straightforward as I imagined in the first place, because I start off with a basic idea, and then see how it works out. Some ideas need a bit more length, and then, of course, there is the problem of making the decision of when something is actually finished! I often feel the need to add a few more paragraphs, and yet sometimes I simply can't think of anything else to add! It never seems to be cut and dried!'

'Well, you've got a lot of work still to go, so I'd better not get in your way! Off you go!'

David set himself to work, and this is the result of that week's work:

Jim Blenkinsop was a trade union shop steward at a big factory in his home town of Nottingham, a factory known throughout the world for the quality of the bicycles it produced. It went almost without saying that a shop steward in such a large factory would also have been elected onto the committee of the local branch of the Labour Party, because the political influence of the trade unions was still extremely strong in those days. There were exceptions however, for he had at least one shop steward colleague who belonged to the Conservative Party; but this was an exception, and Jim belonged to the 'red in tooth and claw' faction of the Labour Party, and, as a matter of principle, would not even acknowledge his Conservative colleague if he happened to meet him in the street. His first wife had also been a party member, but she had died in her late forties; loneliness and sexual attraction had been sufficient to suppress his blinkered politics to such an extent that, when he married again, he chose a woman whose political outlook was far to the right of his, although Jacqueline, his new wife, did not take politics half as seriously as her new husband did.

This caused a certain amount of trouble almost right away, for, before their marriage, they had never seriously discussed politics and, when they ultimately did, Jacqueline took exception to Jim's tendency to dismiss every Conservative voter — or even every Conservative sympathiser – as 'privileged scum' – although he frequently used far more dismissive terms than that to describe them. It was a fundamental facet of Jacqueline's philosophy that she judged everyone as an individual, refusing point blank to consign a whole section of society to the scrap heap just because they had a different point of view, but Jim appeared to be satisfied with finding a label for someone, and then treating them as he would treat everybody to whom he attached that label.

Unfortunately – or so Jim considered it – Jacqueline's view of politics came to be accepted by Jim's son Ted, who had been only fifteen at the time of his mother's death; not so his daughter Jean, who was one year older than Ted, roughly the same age as Jacqueline's daughter, Emily, for Jean's political outlook was similar to that of her father's, which meant that Ted, who had done A Levels at a Sixth Form College and gone on from there to one of the big colleges of the University of London, was regarded by both sister and father as having 'sold out' and turned his back, in their view, on his working-class heritage. Worse was to come, however, for, after university, Ted had opted to become an accountant, a profession which his father inevitably considered as 'stuck up' and 'posh', which meant that henceforth his views on both politics and ethics could safely be disregarded, which led to a certain amount of animosity between father and son. Needless to say, Jim immediately dismissed the view that Ted expressed in the course of one of their disagreements to the effect that his father, in marrying the conservative Jacqueline, had 'sold out' just as much as he had himself in choosing accountancy as his new career; that he did not hold that view too seriously, however, was suggested by Ted's choice of girlfriend, for she, Eileen, was as left-wing in her political views as was Jim.

One evening, Jacqueline suggested to Jim that in a couple of weeks or so they might go to a production at Nottingham Playhouse in a couple of weeks' time; theatre-going was not normally to Jim's taste, but this particular production was of a play by George Bernard Shaw, who, as a red-blooded socialist in Jim's eyes, was therefore at least worthy of consideration. But when she told him which date she had in mind, he reminded her that, as far he was concerned, that would be impossible, because that would be during the week of the Labour Party Conference, and for the whole of that week, therefore, he would naturally be in Blackpool.

Jacqueline had already bought a pair of theatre tickets, not even dreaming that her husband would be away that week, and not even realising that it might clash with the Party Conference, for party conferences did not loom as large in her life as they did in Jim's. This was despite the fact that he had attended the Conference every year since they had married, and that it was always held on roughly the same date. So she suggested to Ted that he and Eileen might like to go to the theatre in their stead.

'Not really up my street, Mum,' he responded, 'I don't really care too much for Shaw, and in any case Eileen is going to the Labour Party Conference in Blackpool that week too.'

A few days later, both Jim and Eileen were at a ward meeting of their local Labour Party, and afterwards, Jim suggested to Eileen that, since the meeting had finished fairly early, she might like to join him in a drink before they returned home. As it had already been arranged that she would have a lift home after the meeting in Jim's car, she accepted, particularly since she had assumed that there would be a number of people in the pub, not just the two of them.

When they arrived at the *White Lion* pub, Jim led her into the Lounge Bar, and offered her a drink; she chose a lemonade, but Jim persuaded her to have a 'proper drink', so she opted for a port and lemon, while Jim chose a light ale. While Jim was at the bar buying the drinks, Eileen looked round the bar, and could see no one she knew; she remarked as much to Jim when he returned with the drinks, but he replied that, if they had gone for a drink, most of the others would have gone to a pretty rough pub, and wouldn't have been seen dead in a posh pub like the *White Lion*.

They started drinking and began talking about some aspects of the meeting they had just attended. After a few minutes Jim pointed out that Eileen's glass was empty, and suggested that she have another, an offer that she declined. When Jim pointed out that, after he had been talking all evening he really needed another drink himself, she changed her mind, and the second one went down even more quickly than the first.

'Same again?' Jim suggested.

Eileen giggled. 'Are you trying to get me drunk?' she said. 'I won't be responsible for anything I do at this rate!'

'Promises, promises!' was Jim's answer, as he got up to get them both another drink.

'You are naughty, Mr Blenkinsop,' said Eileen, raising her third port and lemon to her lips.

'I know,' he replied, 'but I don't mind if you don't!' – at which she just giggled. 'I think you're really beautiful, Eileen,' he went on.

'Do you really?' she replied.

'Oh God, yes, I do!' he said, placing his hand on her leg under the table, to which, he was relieved to find, she did not appear to object.

A few minutes later they walked out of the pub into the car park, and kissed when they got into the car, after which Jim invited her to join him on the back seat, an invitation which she accepted quite readily, and there, in a dark corner of the car park, they made love before Jim drove her home.

Before she got out of the car, he kissed her again, and then asked, 'Have you done anything like that with Ted yet?'

'No,' she said, 'I wouldn't mind, but he says that sort of thing has got to wait until we're married.'

'Chump!' he commented. 'No wonder he's a Tory! But don't worry, his father's got red blood running through his veins!'

Over the next few weeks, Jim and Eileen saw each other several times after work; for the benefit of Jacqueline, Jim invented a minor industrial dispute at the factory in order to explain his working late, whilst Eileen told Ted that she had been asked to work overtime in the large department store in Nottingham city centre where she had been working ever since she left school, because it had been decided that the shop would remain open until eight o'clock one evening a week.

At an early stage in their relationship too, Jim and Eileen had agreed that they would share a hotel room in Blackpool when the annual Labour Party conference came round. As local delegates to the Conference, each of them was able to claim hotel expenses, and Jim had suggested to Eileen that if they shared a hotel room, they could each claim for a single room and thus make a tidy profit on the transaction.

Eileen was not difficult to persuade; her only reservation was that the Conference proceedings would be shown each day on national television, her worry being that either Jacqueline or Ted would happen to switch on and catch sight of them sitting together. Jim quickly reassured her by saying that, given their political views, neither his wife nor Eileen's boyfriend would be likely to switch on the coverage; and if they did, they would be able to explain their sitting together quite easily by saying that all the local delegations sat together as a matter of course. He also explained that if they travelled together in his car, Eileen would still be able to make quite a large profit by claiming the train fare from Nottingham to Blackpool.

All might have gone smoothly for Eileen and Jim if Ted had been readier to accept without question his girlfriend's sudden willingness to work overtime in the store, for, on a previous occasion when overtime had been mentioned, she had turned it down on the grounds that it would mean that Ted and she would be able to spend less time together.

But one evening when she was supposedly working late in the store, Ted decided to go into town and visit the shop where she worked; to his surprise, he found the doors of the store locked. Moreover, when he looked at the notice on the doors listing the opening hours of the shop, he found that there was no mention of late opening on any day of the week.

His suspicions aroused, he went to the store just before one o'clock on a Thursday, which was listed as early closing day, and he saw her leaving the shop on the stroke of one, then standing still for a minute, as if looking for someone; he stayed for a few minutes where she would not have been able to see him, and then, to his surprise, he observed his father's car pull up outside the entrance to the shop, whereupon Eileen immediately got into the passenger's seat, kissed Jim passionately, and the car immediately disappeared from sight.

Ted was furious, but decided to say nothing to either his father or to Eileen for the time being, partly because he could not believe that his father would have an affair with his girlfriend, and partly because he found it even less credible that Eileen could be attracted by a man old enough to be her father, or his father come to that, and partly because, in the two or three weeks before the Party Conference, his father maintained that he was so busy that he spent hardly any time at home. The same was true for Eileen, or at least she claimed it was, and Ted saw very little of Eileen for over a fortnight.

The next time he saw her was, in fact, the very next day, when he did very little else apart from fretting over what he had witnessed as Eileen left work the previous day. So he decided to go to the store where she worked just before closing time. He stood in the precise spot where he had stood on the Thursday, and was soon rewarded with the sight of his girlfriend leaving the shop. As before, she stood and looked around, and two minutes later Ted's father's car came round the corner, she got into the car, the pair embraced, and within seconds the car was nowhere to be seen. 'Right then, you dirty old man,' thought Ted, 'I'll get even with you!'

When Ted arrived home half an hour later, his mother was just setting the table for supper; he noticed too that she was setting only four places instead of the normal five. 'Mum,' he said, 'who's not eating tonight?'

'Oh dear, are you feeling hungry, Ted? I think there'll be plenty to eat for you, don't worry!' – deciding to treat Ted's question as a joking matter instead of revealing to him that she was peeved because her father had only telephoned home an hour before, to let her know that he would not be home for supper himself. 'There's only going to be you and me and the two girls this evening, because your dad's got so much work on with the Party Conference taking place next week.'

'Oh, right,' replied Ted, who had also decided not to reveal exactly what he imagined his father's work would consist of that evening. 'Is there anything I can do?'

'No, I don't think so,' came the reply. 'Are you going out with Eileen tonight?'

'No, I'm afraid not, Eileen's got too much work as well.'

'Oh, okay, just go and wash your hands then. We're eating a bit early this evening because Jean and Emily are going out.'

'Where are they going to then?'

'I think they're going to a dance, so you and I will have to keep each other company while the two girls go out enjoying themselves, and your dad and Eileen are busy working.'

'Okay, shan't be a minute,' said Ted, refraining from voicing the thought that came into his head that it was not just his two sisters who would be bent on pleasure that evening...

When Ted's father came home, Ted did his best to avoid seeing him, and made sure over the weekend that he did not find himself alone with him either. His mind was fully occupied with the notion of taking revenge; all that was needed now was to decide exactly what form his revenge would take, and he felt that having a row with either his dad or Eileen would cancel out any satisfaction that revenge might provide him with.

Ted did not have to wait until the weekend was over before his father provided him with a clue as to how he might take revenge. It was during Sunday evening's supper that the occasion arose, when Jim suddenly announced that he would be travelling by car to Blackpool the following weekend.

Jacqueline appeared surprised. 'Oh,' she said, 'you don't usually take the car when you go to Conference.'

'No,' replied Jim, 'but it's a long way away this time.'

'I would have thought that was a good reason to go by train,' said Jacqueline. 'You've always travelled by train when it's been in Blackpool before…'

'Ah yes, but this time Ted's Eileen will be going too, and I know she's not very well off, so I offered to take her by car, then she won't have to shell out the train fare beforehand.'

'Don't you get travel expenses then?' asked Ted, although he knew the answer already.

'Yes, of course we do,' said Jim, 'but it sometimes takes several weeks before the travel expenses are actually paid.'

'And will you both be able to claim First Class rail travel then?' Ted asked.

'No, unfortunately,' replied his father, 'it's only because I'm a Shop Steward that I have the right to claim that. Eileen will get Second Class fare.'

'Sounds very democratic!' Ted commented.

Jim started to defend this inequality of treatment in a political party which prided itself on being 'democratic', but he was interrupted by his wife, whose agenda was not quite on the same wavelength as her son's. 'And when are you travelling then?' she said. 'I'm sure you'll have the Friday off anyway, because you're a

Shop Steward, but I'm positive Eileen won't be able to get the day off from the shop!'

'No, she's fixed it already. They're okay with it.'

'Really? And are you okay with it, Ted?'

'I didn't know anything about it before, but it looks as if I'm going to have to be okay with it, doesn't it?'

With that, Ted got up, left the table and went out, preferring to keep his powder dry.

In the course of the next few days, just before the Party Conference began on the Saturday, Ted did a lot of research with a view to exacting his revenge in the most effective way possible, but he still refrained from mentioning the matter to Eileen or to his father. On the Friday, however, when Jim and Eileen were already well on their road to Blackpool, he telephoned the police, and managed to arrange a meeting with a senior representative of the Fraud Squad.

Armed with as much evidence as he could muster, he went to Sherwood Lodge, the headquarters of the Nottinghamshire County Police, travelling by bus, which meant undertaking a complicated journey from his home on the Clifton Estate, involving several bus routes. He arrived just in time for his two o'clock appointment, and was shown into a room where, after a five minute wait, a young man not much older than he was himself came in and introduced himself as Inspector Donaldson.

'How can I help you, Mr Wilson?'

Ted told him that he was an accountant, and that he had come across what appeared to him as falsely claiming expenses. He explained the circumstances without identifying the parties concerned, fearing that it would damage his case if he revealed that the main person involved was his father, and that his father's chief accomplice was his girlfriend. He had even sought out the details of the travel and subsistence allowances that his father would be likely to claim, what rail fares he would be eligible to claim, and what his journey would be likely to cost him in reality, given the type of car he drove; here again he provided full details. His figures revealed that his father would be likely to benefit from his fraud by not much less than a thousand pounds.

'Mr Wilson,' Inspector Donaldson said, 'thank you for setting out your allegations with such clarity, but, although nine hundred odd pounds might appear to be quite a lot of money, I have to say that if we were to take on a case such as this, it would involve spending far more money from public funds than it would recoup. Moreover, if we reacted to every case of fiddling of expenses that we get wind of, we would probably find ourselves arresting most public servants, and most of our colleagues too.'

'What?' Ted exploded. 'Are you telling me that the whole of society is corrupt? That's appalling!'

'To say that the whole of society is corrupt would be going a bit far, sir,' said the inspector, 'but in truth we have to judge what we might gain from pursuing any given case, and from what you have told me, what we would gain from this would be very small, so small as to be insignificant. But please leave your documents with me, and my colleagues and I will have a look at them again, and if we do decide to act, I will be in touch.'

'Okay,' said Ted, rather disappointed. 'Here you are.'

The inspector glanced at the documents briefly as Ted passed them to him. 'Oh,' he said, 'I've just noticed that the person you are informing upon is also named Wilson. Is he any relation at all?'

'Yes, he's my father,' Ted admitted.

'And the woman?'

'She's my girlfriend.'

'Given those circumstances, Mr Wilson, I'm afraid I have to say there is really very little chance of our taking action. Let me explain. If it were to come to court, for instance, you would have to be called as a witness, and the lawyers acting for the defence would undoubtedly have a very strong defence in alleging that the motivation for bringing the case had more to do with sexual jealousy than with actual fraud, I'm sorry. Is sexual jealousy involved?'

'Of course it bloody is!' Ted shouted. 'What young man wouldn't react like that when he finds that his dad is sleeping with his girlfriend?'

'I'm sorry, sir, but that's domestic, it's not fraud. It's all part of normal life, I'm afraid. It's not very nice for you, but what they are doing is not actually a crime! Well, technically, I suppose, they are involved in a sort of fraud, but on a very small scale, and if we followed that up, we wouldn't have the resources to follow up on the really big cases.'

'I see,' said Ted, 'and I do understand. I'm sorry I reacted the way I did.'

'That's understandable,' said Inspector Donaldson. 'Thank you for coming in.'

So saying, he shook Ted by the hand, and then Ted had to make the complicated bus journey again, but this time in reverse.

By the time Ted returned home, his father, and also Eileen, he assumed, had set off for Blackpool.

As it happened, Emily and Jean, Ted's two sisters, were also out for the evening, leaving Ted and his step-mother Jacqueline alone to have their evening meal together.

Ted had already thought about the conversation he would have with Jacqueline, providing he was able to get her on her own for a few moments; now, however, he found himself not only alone with her but with far more time at their disposal than he had imagined.

The first decision he took was that he would say nothing to Jacqueline about what he was convinced was her husband's infidelity, not because he felt embarrassed, but because he simply thought it was not the sort of thing that a stepson should discuss with his stepmother. Strangely, he felt on safer ground when it came to the matter of his having reported his father to the fraud squad, partly because he felt less emotional about it, partly because, as an accountant, he possessed an almost evangelical zeal in his opposition to any kind of fraud; he was deceiving himself, however, if he really believed that his judgment on that matter was totally unclouded by emotion.

At Jacqueline's invitation he sat at the table while she brought the meal in from the kitchen; as he waited, his mind was occupied by thoughts of the best way in which he might introduce the subject. Should he launch straight into it, saying something like, 'I've informed the police that Dad has been fiddling his expenses', or try a slightly more casual entry: 'By the way, I've been to the police headquarters this afternoon, and I mentioned to them that my dad has been fiddling his expenses...'

But he did neither, for it was Jacqueline who opened their conversation: 'So what do you think about your Dad pinching your girlfriend, Ted?'

This was a bombshell indeed, the last thing he was expecting. Without thinking about the various constructions that one might put on Jacqueline's question, he replied immediately, and from the very heart of his being.

'He can have her for all I care! She's finished as far as I'm concerned!'

Jacqueline was shaken. 'That's a bit extreme, isn't it? They've only gone off to a conference together, when all's said and done!'

'Oh, have they? You think that, do you?'

'Well, I *was* thinking that! Do you know something that I don't then?'

'I don't know what you don't know...'

'Well, I know that they're both going to the same conference, and that they're travelling in the same car...'

'But you said something about Dad pinching my girlfriend!'

'I didn't mean it like that! It was only a light-hearted way of putting it.'

'It didn't seem light-hearted to me...'

Jacqueline looked at Ted and could see that he was deeply upset. 'Look,' she said, 'I can see you're really upset about something. Are you upset because of the form of words I used, or is there something serious behind it? You are upset, aren't you?'

'Yes, I am,' he admitted, 'and it wasn't just the expression you used either!'

'Now look, Ted, are you upset, or angry?'

'Both!'

'Why?'

'Because I really do think that Dad has pinched my girlfriend. It didn't occur to me that you didn't really mean it.'

'But you must have some reason for thinking that. What's happened?'

'I didn't mean to say anything about it to you, but when you started talking about Dad pinching my girlfriend I thought you already knew about it...'

'Already knew about what? I don't know anything.'

'Well, just forget that I said anything.'

'I can't! You seem to be making a serious allegation, Ted! You must tell me! If there's something going on, I want to know about it...'

'If you think I'm making a serious allegation, that's because I am! Well, a few weeks ago, Elaine told me she wouldn't be able to see me that evening because she'd got to work late at the shop. It so happened that I was walking past her shop at closing time – the normal closing time, that is – and I saw her come out. Then Dad's car turned up, she got in, and she kissed him.'

'She kissed him? You mean just on the cheek?'

'No, a proper kiss, a really passionate one! Then they drove off. And that wasn't the only time either. I've seen her going off in his car three or four times.'

'Have you now! And have you mentioned it to her?'

'No, I haven't said a word. Actually, I haven't really had a chance, because I've hardly seen her since the first time I saw her get into his car.'

'And are you planning to speak to her about it when she gets back from Blackpool?'

'Too right I am! I'm going to tell her it's all over between us. It never occurred to me that she was that sort of girl...'

'What sort of girl?'

'A slut.'

'That's a hard word!'

'But if she's been carrying on with my dad in the way that I think she has, I don't think it is too harsh a word. But you don't seem to be upset by what's going on! I thought you'd be much more upset than that!'

'If it turns out that you're right, then I will be upset. But then I haven't seen any evidence myself, and until I do have any, I'd prefer to hold fire for a while.'

'Fair enough. But there's something else as well...'

'What's that?'

'I think he's fiddling his expenses, and I've told the police about it.'

'You've done what?'

'I've been talking to the Fraud Squad.'

'And do you have any evidence?'

'Not hard evidence, because there isn't any yet, but there will be as soon as he puts in his expenses claim. But you heard what he was saying about it the other week...'

'I don't remember.'

'It was when he announced that he was going to Blackpool by car, and he was talking about the fact that he could claim First Class rail fare and Eileen could claim Second Class rail fare, and...'

'Oh, I remember now... But I don't remember there being anything that would justify informing the Fraud Squad!'

'Perhaps I was allowing the fact that I was upset because I'd obviously misjudged Eileen so badly to influence my thinking. But it's done now...'

'And now the Fraud Squad will be calling on him, will they?'

'I don't know. I've left some documents with them, and they say they'll examine them...'

'Well, let's wait and see. Until I know something definite I'd prefer to suspend judgment, I think.'

'That's your right. I have no problem with that.'

In the meantime, Jim and Eileen had arrived in Blackpool, where they had checked into a guest house just outside the town, not simply because they wanted to avoid bumping into anybody else from the conference, but because nearly all of the hotels where most of the delegates stayed had negotiated 'special conference' terms, which tied in pretty well with the Party subsistence allowance, whereas, at the guest house which Jim had booked, they would actually make much more profit, since the charges were substantially below what they would be able to claim back.

When they checked in, Eileen was pleased to note that Jim had checked them in as 'Mr and Mrs Blenkinsop': for some time now, she had been contemplating that she would eventually bear the name of 'Mrs Blenkinsop', although she had previously imagined that it would be as Mrs Edward Blenkinsop, not Mrs James Blenkinsop, and she had always assumed that her husband would be considerably younger than the man with whom she was intending to spend the next few nights.

As soon as they found themselves alone in the double bedroom which Jim had reserved, Eileen said, 'As you've checked me in as Mrs James Blenkinsop, I assume that you'll be wanting to claim your conjugal rights straight away, will you?'

'I can't think of anything I'd like better,' said Jim. 'I'm afraid my mind has been fixed on that ever since we drove out of Nottingham! How do you feel?'

'I thought you'd been thinking of that,' she replied. 'There was an expression on your face every time you looked at me that made me think of that too!'

'So is that all right with you, Eileen?'

'I'd got the impression that that was the whole object of the exercise! So come on then!' she said flirtatiously, as she started to remove her blouse.

Half an hour later, still lying in bed, Jim suddenly said, 'Tell me, do you feel guilty at all about what we've just done?'

'Because of Ted, you mean? No, not at all! Do you?'

'No, certainly not! We're consenting adults, after all, aren't we?'

'Well, I consent anyway, and you certainly didn't seem reluctant!'

'I'm not! Not in the slightest! But I keep thinking about our future relationship...'

'What do you mean?'

'Well, I mean, I always imagined that you would get married to Ted...'

'Yes, that's the plan. But if you think that after I've married Ted I'm still going to have sex with you, you've got another think coming!'

'Why not?'

'Well, I seem to remember there's something in the marriage service which involves me promising to keep myself only unto him...'

'And are you really going to marry him?'

'Well, everybody assumes that he and I are an item now, so I expect we will.'

'And knowing that you're going to marry my son, you still want to have sex with me?'

'Oh yes! Because he won't have sex with me until we're married, and I rather like sex, haven't you noticed?'

'I've noticed!'

'And what about you? Do you feel guilty about Jacqueline?'

'A bit. But I like being with you too!'

'Have you told her that we're sharing a room... sharing a bed, I mean?'

'I certainly haven't! I haven't even told her we're staying in the same hotel!'

'Why not?'

'Well, have you told Ted?'

'Certainly not!'

'So I can ask you the same question. Why not?'

'Because he's too strait-laced. Anyway, we're not here to talk about our other halves, are we? As long as we're here, I'm all yours, so there!'

'I'm glad of that!'

Some time later, Jim and Eileen showered and changed, then went down to have their evening meal, but, because the guest house had no licence to sell alcohol, they went out afterwards to a pub for a couple of drinks, before returning to the guest house for an early night. Well, it was still early when they both got into bed...

Eventually they went to sleep, but, around two o'clock in the morning, Jim's mobile phone started ringing. He reached out for it wearily, switched it on and said, 'Hello.'

'Are you listening?' he heard a female voice say.

'Yes, I'm listening,' he replied.

'This is very important,' said the voice, which sounded exactly like Jacqueline's. 'I did not call the police.'

'What do you mean?' he asked.

'I did not call the police,' the voice repeated. 'It was your family that called the police.'

'Whatever are you talking about?' asked Jim. 'Jacqueline, is that Jacqueline?' But there was no answer; the caller had rung off.

'Who are you talking to?' asked a sleepy Eileen.

'I don't know,' replied Jim, 'but it sounded like Jacqueline. But I don't think it could have been her.'

'Why not?'

'Because of what she said.'

'So what did she say?'

'She said she had not called the police. It was my family that had called the police.'

'What did she mean?'

'I have no idea!'

'Did you ask her to explain?'

'Yes, I did, but she just rang off.'

But Eileen, satisfied that Jacqueline's call had not been prompted by the fact that she had learned of her husband's infidelity, had already gone to sleep again. Jim tried to follow suit, but less successfully, for his mind was seriously troubled by the call he had received, whoever it was from, and it was an hour later that he was able to drop off once more.

The following morning he and Eileen talked about it again over breakfast. 'If that call really was meant for you,' she asked, 'is there any reason why you should be worried about somebody reporting you to the police?'

'No, not at all. I've not done anything illegal as far as I'm aware!'

'You were very naughty last night!' Eileen said skittishly.

'I know, and so were you! But we didn't do anything the police would be interested in!'

'Then stop worrying about it! It obviously wasn't Jacqueline, and it must have been a wrong number! What number was it from, have you looked?'

'Yes, I have looked, but the number was withheld. But what if Jacqueline has found out about us?'

'If she has found out about us, she wouldn't have called the police! In any case, if she does know, then Ted will soon know as well, and I will probably get a call from him too!'

'And so will I! So if we don't hear anything from Ted in the next couple of hours, say, we should be in the clear!'

But three hours later, neither of them had received a call from anyone, be it Ted, Jacqueline, or the police, so they both came to the conclusion that nothing more would come of it, and they had nothing to worry about.

Back in Nottingham, Jacqueline too was thinking about the phone call she had made. Prompted by Ted's having told her that he had reported his father to the police, her desire had been merely to worry her husband and to disturb him, in which, of course, she had been successful. To a certain extent she was concerned that she had perhaps not been specific enough in her challenge, but in truth she was in possession of very few of the facts of the case, so it would have been impossible to be much more specific. On the other hand she also wondered whether she had been wise to make the call herself; she had, of course, taken a conscious decision to make it a cryptic message, precisely because her object was to make her errant husband anxious. So now she took another conscious decision: not to say anything to Ted about the phone call she had made, basically because she was rather embarrassed about it.

As she was busying herself with preparing lunch, however, the kitchen door opened, and her stepson Ted appeared. 'I was wondering if you'd got the lunchtime news on TV?' he asked.

'No, I haven't,' she answered. 'Why?'

'Because they've just shown a clip from the Labour Party Conference, and there, in the audience, I saw Dad, sitting next to Eileen!'

'That doesn't prove anything!' she said. 'We knew they were going to the conference together, and it's not really surprising that they should sit together, is it?'

'I suppose it isn't. But I don't like them being there at all.'

'But that's a different matter entirely! The BBC are hardly likely to put pictures of them in bed together on TV, are they? And it would need something like that to prove that your suspicions are correct!'

'I suppose you're right. Perhaps I'm just being neurotic...'

'There's no crime in that. But if they have been getting up to what you suspect, at least you've found out in time what she's like. It's about ten years too late for me to find out about him though!'

'That's true, I'm afraid. I'm sorry, Mum!'

'And what about you and Eileen? Are you really going to give her up then?'

'My instinct tells me I should! What about you and Dad?'

'My instinct tells me I should too, but common sense tells me to grow up!'

'What do you mean?'

'Given that there are two alternatives, I mean that I need to calculate which alternative would lead to the larger profit, or the larger loss. And I think I might have more to lose by ditching your dad!'

'But look what he's done to you!'

'Exactly! Let's just look at what he's done to me. He's taken a fancy to a young girl, and he gave in. He was discreet, he didn't throw it in my face, and in a few days' time he'll be coming home to me. And if I say nothing, the chances are that he'll say nothing too, and if there's no bad blood, where's the harm?'

'But what if he enjoyed the experience so much he goes off with someone else and does it again?'

'Then I will have learnt another lesson! But I'll be on firmer ground, because I shall know that I've forgiven him once.'

'I don't think I could do that.'

'Why not?'

'Because making love is an intimate, sacred thing.'

'Intimate yes, sacred no, I would say. I'm going to ask you a very intimate question, Ted, a question I have no right to ask...'

'I know what your question is, and the answer is no!'

'And you have never wanted to?'

'Oh yes, of course I have, but I believe it should only take place in the context of a marriage.'

'Does she believe that too?'

'Obviously not!'

'And how do you know that you're right and she's wrong?'

'An awful lot of people believe that too...'

‘An awful lot of people believe in capital punishment. Does that mean you do?’

‘No, of course not!’

‘Why not?’

‘Because capital punishment is barbaric!’

‘That means that an awful lot of people are barbaric! If you believe in following the crowd, you’d believe in capital punishment!’

‘I don’t believe in following the crowd.’

‘But in sexual matters you do…’

‘No, I don’t! It would be too easy to give in to…’

‘To the flesh, you mean?’

‘Yes.’

‘But a lot of people would say that’s only human. Do you want a wife that’s not human?’

‘Oh, of course not, you’re tying me up in knots!’

‘I’m sorry, I wasn’t intending to, I was just trying to help you see the path ahead more clearly. Let’s retrace our steps a bit. You said that you’ve wanted to have sex with Eileen, but you’ve stopped yourself. Is that right?’

‘Yes.’

‘And has Eileen ever wanted to have sex with you?’

‘Yes.’

‘And she’s stopped herself too?’

‘Not exactly.’

‘What do you mean by that?’

‘I’ve stopped her.’

‘What!’

‘I’ve stopped her. It’s a moral thing.’

'So when it comes to moral things, it's your word that counts, is it? Is that fair? How do you think that must make her feel?'

'I don't know.'

'Well, I think you should think things through properly before you make a life-changing decision, don't you?'

'I suppose that makes sense, yes.'

'So think things over properly...'

'Okay, Mum.'

So Ted went and thought things over, and so did Jacqueline, because in her questioning of her stepson she had also been questioning herself, and the ultimate outcome was that Ted married Eileen and that Jacqueline stayed with Jim. It would be ridiculous to suggest that they all lived happily after, because that rarely happens in real life, but they each at least achieved relative happiness and contentment, and, for the rest of his life, Jim only occasionally wondered about the mysterious phone call that had come at dead of night, and whether the police would come knocking on his door in the morning.

'Well, well,' said Margaret as soon as she had finished reading David's story, 'that's a raunchy one, and no mistake! And it looks as if you're a convert to the idea of free love!'

'No, I'm not! I could have just as easily taken the puritan way out, but I chose to have them follow the path of pragmatism.'

'Why?'

'Because fewer people get hurt that way!'

'But it's only fiction, isn't it? What does it matter if a few people get hurt?'

'When I've created a set of characters, they're real people to me, and on the whole I try not to make them suffer. It's impossible to do that all the time obviously, but they do matter to me. And in any case, an author isn't obliged to agree with everything his characters say, or approve of everything they say.'

'I know that – you've told me that often enough before! So do you really believe that errant other halves should be allowed to get away with it?'

'I believe the same answer applies! And in any case, Ted and Eileen knew very well what they were doing, and if they really felt guilty about it, their continued guilt will be their eternal punishment! After all, that's what guilt does...'

Chapter Eight

The next Monday morning, David and Margaret sat having breakfast together.

'I'm not going to ask you my usual Monday morning question...' said Margaret.

'Oh, what's that then?'

'You should know already! I usually ask you what your plans are for your next chapter.'

'So why aren't you going to ask me today?'

'Because I'm fed up with getting the same answer.'

'Which is?'

'You usually say that you've got no idea!'

'Well, for once I do have! The only thing is, it's something that's been in my mind since the very start, and I've been putting it off and putting it off until I'm absolutely terrified of making a start!'

'Well, you'd better tell me what it's about then!'

'Well, I reckon I have two chapters still to write. The last one, of course, will be the answer to the whole riddle, and as yet I don't have a clue about that! The other one, which I've been putting off is something I'm not very keen on writing about, in fact I'm not very keen about even thinking about it!'

'So what is it?'

'I don't like to say...'

'Oh, go on...'

'It's something very nasty, and it's one of the very first ideas I came up with. It's blackmail...'

'That is a nasty subject, I agree. Have you chosen a particular blackmailer?'

'I've invented one, and she's a nasty piece of work too!'

'I see, so there's going to be another nasty woman is there? I'm beginning to suspect you've got something against women, you know!'

'Well, her victims are usually male, and they sometimes come off worse off than she does.'

'Okay, but it's got to be good!'

'I think it will be... I've been mulling it over in my mind for weeks and weeks!'

'So you'd better get on with it then!'

'That's what you always say! Okay, I'm off...'

So David set himself to writing, and this is what he wrote:

Blackmail is an ugly word, and an even uglier phenomenon, which brings misery to its victims and dishonour to its perpetrator.

I have often wondered what blackness of mood is so sinister as to compel an individual to succumb to the temptation to commit so heinous a crime. Need, after all, can lead to theft, as when genuine hardship or poverty, or the inability to provide for one's dependents, can persuade a person to feel such desperation that they cannot resist the temptation to resort to that particular crime. Jealousy too can cause such intense anger that it may ultimately lead to murder, compelling somebody to deprive someone else of their very being, whilst hopelessness, born of an inability to make one's way in the world despite one's very best efforts, can incite people to risk their lives in order to get to another country, or else harbour thoughts of revolution with all its bloody consequences. But what drives a blackmailer? Poverty, envy and despair seem inadequate motives; it seems to me that nothing less than a combination of several of the Seven Deadly Sins would be sufficient to drive someone to that particular degradation.

Blanche Delaney was a woman who, in everyone else's mind, had everything: looks, riches, intellect, influence and power, but, it would appear, that was not enough. She was also a blackmailer, and a blackmailer of the most vicious kind, said the judge at her trial, before sentencing her to fourteen years' imprisonment, the maximum sentence allowed by the law.

But she had not always been a blackmailer, although, in her early years, she was already showing little sign of caring what effect her words or deeds might have on those at whom they were directed; in short, she seemed totally devoid of conscience. In theory at least, it should not have been so, for her father was an Anglican priest and her mother was well known for her charitable work, both formally, in that she worked for one of the internationally known charitable organisations, and informally, in that she could always be relied upon to lend a hand wherever a hand was needed. Perhaps her parents made unreasonable demands of her, or maybe she herself did not feel sufficiently adequate to be able to cope with her parents' – and everyone else's – expectations. Who knows? Before her trial she was subjected to innumerable investigations and tests by psychiatrists, but, although theories and speculations as to her state of mind were many, true facts were few.

The first instance of her unwelcome intrusion into another individual's private life was, in truth, fairly trivial, and it arose from boredom – or, in terms of the Seven Deadly Sins, sloth.

She was in her late twenties at the time, and had no regular boyfriend, although her suitors were many. One evening she had agreed to go out with one of them for dinner, to be followed by a visit to a nightclub, but he had pulled out at the last minute, leaving her with nothing to do that evening but eat alone in her apartment and speak to friends on the telephone. She had spoken to three of her friends already by nine o'clock, at which time she phoned a former school friend by the name of Clarissa.

'Hello, Clarissa,' said Blanche when her friend picked up the phone. 'It's Blanche speaking, and I'm feeling utterly fed up – nowhere to go to, and no one to go with!'

'Oh,' replied Clarissa, who was especially surprised because she had originally been supposed to be going out with Blanche that evening, but discovered only the previous evening that their planned evening out was cancelled because her friend had been invited out by 'the most divine man'. 'So what happened to your date?' she continued.

'He stood me up, the rat!' said Blanche. 'He phoned me at about four o'clock this afternoon to say that he couldn't make it after all, and he didn't even tell me a reason! I'm so unhappy!'

'Who were you supposed to be going out with? Do I know him?'

'I don't know whether you know him or not. His name is Edward Playfair.'

'Oh, him! I should steer clear of him if I were you! Playing fair is the last thing on his mind!'

'Oh! Thanks for the warning. I can't believe that he couldn't be bothered to invent a reason!'

'He probably didn't want to, or didn't dare to! The most likely reason would be that his wife had other plans for the evening...'

'His wife! Is he married then?'

'Oh yes, didn't you know? He's been married for years, but he still likes to play the field!'

Blanche, whose disposition was totally opposed to viewing herself as 'one of the field', felt extremely peeved. 'No, I didn't know he was married! What a cad he must be! If I'd known that, I certainly wouldn't have agreed to go out with him!'

Clarissa smiled to herself, for she was well aware that Blanche had previously been out with any number of married men, and had even confessed to her that, as long as she had a good time, she couldn't care less whether they were married or not. 'I know. The moment you told me he was the most divine man, I thought of all the stories we were told when we were at Roedean about the Greek gods and the naughty things they used to get up to!'

'Oh yes, not that we were ever told what they really got up to!'

'No, of course, the mistresses left it up to our imagination!'

'Yes, and our imaginations were so active that our version of the myths was highly exaggerated!'

The phone call lasted only another two or three minutes, for Blanche was feeling very angry, not just because Edward had stood her up, but also because she was convinced that her friend Clarissa was secretly laughing at her, whilst pretending to be sympathetic to her plight.

When Blanche had rung off, she poured herself a large gin and tonic and then sat musing over her predicament, such as it was, for Blanche had never been known to refuse to look on the black side of life. After two hours and two more gin and tonics her thoughts turned to considering the best way to take her revenge on Edward for his callousness. Not that she was seriously angry with him, for the entire set she moved in would probably have behaved in exactly the same way; it was more a matter of thoughts suddenly coming into her head simply because she felt she had nothing to do.

Eventually she went to bed, but slept only fitfully. Just after two o'clock she suddenly woke up and thought of a way to get back at Edward: she would telephone him, there and then...

For a moment she hesitated. She had already decided what to say to him, but what if it were his wife who answered the phone? Even worse, what if it turned out that his wife were someone she knew?

In a matter of seconds she dismissed her reservations, trusting in her ability to find something suitably hurtful to say if something unexpected were to present itself. She dialled Edward's number, heard the ringing tone and then Edward's voice:

'Hello, who's that?'

Ignoring his request to identify herself, Blanche continued: 'Are you listening?'

There followed a few seconds of silence, so she repeated: 'Are you listening?'

'Oh yes,' he replied.

'This is very important. I did not call the police. It was your family that called the police.'

'What the devil are you talking about? Who is that?' Edward responded in an agitated fashion.

Satisfied that he did not know who was calling and that he seemed upset, Blanche replaced the receiver, leaving Edward to ponder over the identity of his caller, the meaning of the message, and to worry over the hidden threat implied by the message.

Why did Blanche say what she said? Simply to make Edward fret. She knew perfectly well that nothing he had done to her would merit a police involvement; but she was also aware that simply telling someone that they have been reported to the police was sufficient to make them feel uneasy, even if they have no reason to fear the police, and frantically worried if they have. In fact she did not know Edward well enough to be aware if he had done anything to interest the police, but if he had, which was possible, it would serve him right for treating her in such a rotten fashion!

The following day, the act of thinking about it in the cold light of day – made absolutely no difference to Blanche's attitude: on the contrary, she still felt extremely angry with Edward, and resolved to phone him again the next night. Once more she waited until two o'clock in the morning, for she felt that at that time of night people would be at their most vulnerable. She heard the phone ring out, and again heard Edward's voice: 'Hello, who's that?'

This time she replied, 'Is your wife there?'

'No,' he answered, 'she's not. Who wants her?'

Blanche decided to ignore his question, and continued, 'Does she know you pursue other women?'

'Who is that? Is that Blanche, by any chance?'

Again she chose not to answer his question, and asked another of her own. 'Can I speak to her?'

'Speak to whom?'

'To your wife.'

'I told you, she's not here.'

'Where is she?'

'In another room.'

'I suppose she's refusing to sleep with you because she knows you've been chasing other women?'

'No, it's not like that at all.'

'Do you mean she knows about your other women?'

'What other women?'

'Blanche, for instance.'

'Who is that?'

Her resolve fortified by a conviction that he still did not know whom he was talking to, she continued, 'Does your wife know about Blanche?'

'No, she doesn't.'

'So how much money would you pay me not to tell her about Blanche? Shall we say £500?'

'Certainly not!'

'£1000 then?'

'I'm not paying you anything! Who is that?'

But Blanche had replaced the receiver and terminated the call.

The following night Blanche phoned Edward again, once more in the middle of the night. When he answered, she said, 'You owe me £1000.'

'Why?' he replied, not knowing what she was talking about, or even who she was.

'To prevent me telling your wife about Blanche.'

'I thought you said £500 last time.'

'It will go up £500 every time you refuse, until you see sense and agree to pay.'

'But I don't even know who you are! How can I pay somebody if I don't know who they are?'

Blanche felt very heartened by his response, for her strategy depended upon his not being aware that it was Blanche herself that was calling. Naturally she had no intention of actually telling Edward's wife, mainly because she did not want to precipitate any retaliation, of whatever kind.

'I shall give you instructions for payment as soon as you agree to pay.'

'And you won't say anything to my wife if I pay you £500?'

'It was £500 yesterday, so it is £1000 today, and it will go up by £500 every day.'

'And after I pay you, you will leave me alone?'

'It depends.'

'On what?'

'Among other things, on whether you tell the police.'

'But you said the other night that the police already knew...'

'I said nothing of the sort. I have not told the police. The police have nothing to do with it.'

She spoke quietly, calmly; Edward's mind was far from quiet or calm, especially when she continued to speak: 'You have ten seconds to decide. After that I shall speak to your wife.'

'No!' he replied, as forcefully as he could while speaking quietly enough for his wife not to overhear from the adjoining bedroom. 'I'll pay!'

'That is very sensible,' she said. 'You will pay £1000 in cash, you will put it in an envelope with the name Edward Playfair on the front, and leave it at the reception desk of the Ritz in Piccadilly. Is that clear?'

'Very clear. And if I do that, you won't say anything to my wife?'

'If you act exactly as I say within twenty-four hours, you have nothing to fear.'

'All right. I will do it tomorrow afternoon.'

Blanche smiled to herself, and replaced the receiver.

Two days later, Blanche went to the Ritz, asked if an envelope addressed to Edward Playfair had been left there for her to pick up. The receptionist handed over an envelope, and Blanche went straight home. Once there, she opened the envelope, and counted twenty £50 notes, and gave a whoop of joy. 'That was easy!' she told herself. 'Perhaps I should have asked for more!'

A week later, despite what she had told him, she contacted him again, because she had discovered what pleasure may be gained as a result of making a victim squirm. As soon as Edward realised that his blackmailer was on the phone again, he protested: 'You promised me that if I paid you £1000 you would not get in touch with me again!'

'I made no such promise! What I said was that if you paid me within twenty-four hours you had nothing to fear. Are you afraid?'

'No,' he replied, principally because he thought it was the best thing to say.

'There you are, you see!' she countered. 'I said you had nothing to fear. Now I need some more money...'

'How much?'

'A thousand.'

'And if I pay, will you give me an assurance that you won't contact me again?'

'Oh yes! There's just one thing...'

'What's that?'

'What if I'm a liar?'

'Then I shall call the police.'

'Just give me the money, and worry later! Same arrangements as before. You remember?'

'I remember.'

She rang off, then the following day she collected the money that he had left once more at the Ritz, after which she never contacted him again.

But within a day or two she found that the pleasure of receiving money with such little effort had worn off, as had the sadistic satisfaction she had experienced as a result of causing so much pain. The only aspect of blackmail which she had not enjoyed had been the potential risk to herself, which would, of course, always be present if she persisted in threatening her own lovers, of which she had many.

It was not long, however, before a different method suggested itself. She had a wide circle of friends, mostly former school companions and their husbands, and, when they met, there was always a lot of gossip about who was sleeping with whom, because they were indeed a promiscuous set. So she sat down one day and wrote a list of the pairings which were currently being talked about by her friends. Her plan was to follow a similar method to the one she had developed over Edward, always threatening the errant husband with telling his wife of his affair.

Blanche had no need of the money she would make from this venture, for not only was she from a wealthy background, she was also a successful businesswoman, who owned a chain of exclusive and expensive boutiques, which made her self-sufficient, even without resorting to her newly acquired occupation. But her motivation was always the sheer pleasure she could derive from making other people's lives a misery. The fact that her friends' husbands were well-heeled and would not miss the odd thousand pounds that keeping their wives ignorant of their peccadilloes would cost them made it easier for her, of course; ironically, that should surely have neutralised the pleasure she felt as a result of taking their money. Within a few weeks she was blackmailing no fewer than six men, who inexplicably were willing to pay up to avoid their wives being made aware of what they were doing.

A few years later, however, when she was enjoying tea in Fortnum and Mason's with Clarissa, her friend startled her by saying, 'Isn't it an awful shock about Letitia's husband?'

'Why? What happened to him?"

'He committed suicide.'

'Oh. I didn't know. What happened?'

'I understand he was cheating on Letitia...'

'That's not usually fatal. He's done that before!'

'I know, but it appears he shot himself, and there was a note found beside his body that he'd written before killing himself.'

'He could hardly have written it after killing himself! What did it say?'

'The note said that he had been carrying on with another woman, and then he had received a number of telephone calls threatening to tell his wife if he didn't pay a sum of money...'

'How much?'

'I don't know. But he went on to say that he couldn't afford to pay, and that he didn't want his wife to find out about his affair.'

'That doesn't make sense! Killing himself is one sure-fire way of guaranteeing that his wife does find out!'

Clarissa was a little nonplussed by Blanche's curious response, but carried on with what she had been going to say anyway. 'He said in the note that he acknowledged that he and Letitia had been going through a bad spell, and as a result of that he'd started a liaison with another woman, and then someone had begun to blackmail him, and the blackmail was the last straw, so he decided to end it all. Isn't that awful?'

'Did he say who the other woman was?'

'I don't know. I doubt it. But fancy somebody blackmailing him! I can't understand how anybody can do such a thing!'

'It's something men who cheat on their wives lay themselves open to.'

'I suppose so. But could you do such a thing? I know I couldn't.'

'I'm sorry, Clarissa, I'm going to have to scoot – I've got somebody coming in to repair the dishwasher at five o'clock.'

With that, she got up and left, leaving Clarissa more and more puzzled by her reaction, and leaving her to settle the bill for tea and champagne too!

When she got home, she got out her list of prospective victims, crossed Letitia's husband off the list, and thought no more about it – or him.

A little later that evening she started to examine the prospective victims' list seriously, and finally settled on Donald McCormack, the husband of Jeannette McCormack, better known by her maiden name of Jeannette McGrath, a successful and popular actress, who had also been at school with Blanche. Donald too was an actor. He and Jeannette had only been married about ten months; they had met while acting in a play, in which they played a compulsively adulterous couple, a role which they appeared to find difficult to escape from. From such details as Blanche had been able to discover, there was a distinct possibility that she could blackmail both of them rather than just the one; it was only the fact that Jeannette had long been familiar with the sound of Blanche's voice, however, and the consequent likelihood of being identified if she did telephone Jeannette, that caused her to restrict her target to Jeannette's husband.

She easily found out the identity of Donald's current companion, an actress named Gigi Caldwell, and resolved to ring Donald that very night. So, at some time between one and two in the morning she dialled his number, and was surprised by what was awaiting her.

'Who the hell's calling me at this ridiculous time of night?' said Donald.

Blanche ignored his question, and continued with her plan. 'I'm surprised you're not with Gigi Caldwell,' she said.

'I've been with her all evening, and who the hell wants to know? Get off the bloody line!'

'I don't suppose your wife knows about Gigi, does she?'

'Of course she bloody does! Keep your filthy nose out!'

'I bet she doesn't know about all the others!'

'Of course she does! Jeannette and I have no secrets from each other, not even who either of us is currently sleeping with! So go away!'

And Donald slammed the receiver down.

Was Blanche discouraged by this hiccup in her plan? Not in the slightest, for, she calculated, there was no point, and no profit either, in blackmailing a partner of a genuinely 'open' marriage. Of course, she had no way of knowing if he had been telling the truth or not, but she simply shrugged her shoulders and consulted her list of potential victims again, in which all those whom she knew to be errant husbands were marked by an asterisk.

Her eyes immediately lit upon one asterisk in particular, against the names of Hermione and Jason Spencer. As was the case with most of the female names on this list, Blanche had been at school with Hermione, although they had never been truly close. Jason, Hermione's husband, had been for the last nine years or so the Conservative Member of Parliament for a constituency in suburban Surrey, an area which was known for its constant rejection of any idea which did not have its roots deep in the nineteenth century, if not earlier. Certainly, Blanche thought, Jason's constituents would disapprove of his adultery, even if they would also be rubbing their hands with glee if they learned of it.

But first she had to do a little research. Fortunately Isabella, one of her closest school chums, lived in the same area as Hermione and Jason, and was one of Jason's constituents, so Blanche phoned her and virtually invited herself to go and spend the following weekend with Isabella, when she proceeded to ply her with endless questions about her MP, whilst, of course, keeping her motivation secret.

'If you're so anxious to find out about Jason,' said Isabella, 'I will invite him and Hermione to dinner on Saturday evening.'

As it happened, Hermione and Jason had no prior engagements, and so Blanche found herself more than amply rewarded for her brazen cheek in inviting herself to Isabella's for the weekend.

At Isabella's suggestion, Blanche actually arrived early on Friday evening. 'I haven't seen you for ages,' she had said, 'and Alistair won't be back from his business trip until Saturday morning, so we'll be able to enjoy a girlie evening together and catch up on what we've both been up to.'

In fact 'girlie evenings' were not really to Blanche's taste, but she went along with the idea because a private conversation with Isabella appeared to be more promising for her secret plans than a formal dinner with her intended victim, for she would be able to ask her friend the sort of direct questions she would not be able to ask Jason on the occasion of their first meeting.

Isabella's idea of a 'girlie evening' involved a light supper and a considerable amount of wine, which suited Blanche's purposes admirably, although she deliberately refrained from even mentioning Jason's name for the first hour of their conversation, which had begun with Isabella telling Blanche about her husband Alistair's job as a hedge fund manager, and in particular about his latest business trip to New York, before exploring more promising territory in the form of gossip about their former schoolmates and their current partners, of which, to Blanche's delight, Isabella seemed to know most of the gory details.

This provided Blanche with the perfect opportunity to begin talking about Jason and Hermione in the same kind of intimate detail, and Blanche jumped at the chance, while concealing the intensity of her interest by her casual, languid tone. 'By comparison with most of our old school friends,' she started, 'Jason and Hermione's marriage must be extremely boring, I suppose...'

'Not on your life,' Isabella responded, 'you don't know the half of it!'

'Oh, all right then, tell me about it.'

'Well, I don't know anything for certain, and I wouldn't dream of saying anything to Hermione about it – she probably doesn't know anyway – but there's been plenty of gossip at the local Conservative Club about the way he treats his female research assistants...'

'Who, I would expect, are not exactly the matronly type...'

Isabella guffawed. 'Absolutely not! I think they're all mini-skirted dolly birds. I wouldn't dream of wearing a mini-skirt when he's around, I'll tell you!'

'Has he tried anything on with you then?'

Isabella looked shocked. 'Oh, no! He wouldn't dare!'

The unkind thought that went through Blanche's mind was that he wouldn't be tempted by Hermione even if she were wearing a mini-skirt, but she thought it better not to express it. 'Oh, I was thinking of wearing a mini for dinner tomorrow evening!'

'I shouldn't if I were you!' said Isabella. 'Especially since I was intending to put you next to him on the table plan.'

Blanche immediate reaction was to resolve that she would indeed wear a mini-skirt; it could turn out to be a useful litmus test of Jason's susceptibilities. 'But tell me more about these research assistants,' she said. 'Have any of them complained about him? And has there been one in particular?'

'I don't know if there has been one in particular, no, but I doubt if there have been any complaints...'

'Why on earth not?'

'I don't know, but I believe there has been a fair turnover of research assistants, and there's been some talk of Jason paying them when they left, to make sure that they don't tell anyone...'

'You mean he gets them to sign a non-disclosure agreement?'

'I don't really know what that means...'

'It means he would be buying their silence once they've stopped working for him...'

'Oh, I see. Yes, that's what I've heard, but of course you can't believe everything you hear!'

'But on the other hand, there's no smoke without fire.'

'I suppose.'

Isabella's reluctance to say anything further on the matter was intended to convey to Blanche that she wanted to end that particular topic of conversation, and Blanche was content to go along with that, for she was happy that she had a potentially fruitful line of inquiry anyway, and Isabella had already confessed that she knew no more.

The following morning, Isabella's husband Alistair arrived from the airport. Blanche had been looking forward to meet him, because the last time she had seen Isabella had been six years previously, and at that time Isabella and Alistair had not yet even met. But Alistair declared himself jet-lagged after his flight from New York and took himself off to bed, saying that otherwise he would risk falling asleep at the dinner table that evening, so Blanche had to postpone getting to know Alistair until the following day: after all, that evening she would have other fish to fry...

At about 7.30 that evening the dinner guests arrived, Jason wearing a dinner suit, as was Alistair, whilst both Hermione and Isabella were wearing elegant, full length dresses. As for Blanche, her dress was elegant enough, but extremely short, especially for her age; it had even crossed her mind that in a day or two Hermione and Isabella might even describe her as 'mutton dressed as lamb', but she did not care, for her choice of dress was intended to attract the attention of one person only, and in that it was certainly successful. During pre-dinner drinks Jason was affability itself, as, indeed, was Alistair, although Blanche hardly noticed Isabella's husband, or indeed the other ladies, for she was undoubtedly on a mission.

Already, while they were eating their first course, Blanche felt Jason's hand brush her knee, not in a way that could not have been construed as accidental, but a few moments later it happened again. Once more the hand was removed almost as soon as it had made contact with her knee, but the third time it happened there could have been no mistaking his intention, for it remained in contact with her flesh for several seconds before being removed, and next time it happened, she made sure that her own hand was on her knee, and she went on to stroke his hand in return, thus making it clear to Jason that his attentions were far from being unwelcome. By the time the main course arrived, it was obvious to both of them that each hand was seeking contact with the other.

In the interval between main course and dessert, Blanche excused herself, got up from the table and went to the bathroom. When she emerged from the bathroom a few moments later, she found Jason waiting outside. 'Blanche,' he said, 'you are so desirable I would like to see you again. Would you like that?'

'I don't think it would be very appropriate,' she replied.

'Well, please let me kiss you, just once.'

She allowed him to kiss her, but her intended short kiss metamorphosed into an extended kiss, and she felt his arms envelop her. At length she pulled away, and said, 'You've made a mess of my lipstick now! I shall have to go back to my room to repair the damage!'

'Can I come to your room too?' he pleaded.

'No, you certainly can't! People will wonder where we've got to! You'd better go back downstairs at once.'

To her surprise he obeyed and went downstairs again; she rejoined the company a few seconds later, and for the remainder of the meal their hands were joined under the table. But, although Blanche had enjoyed his kiss, the gratification she sought was different, for she was storing up evidence to use against him: for her, mere sexuality had been transformed into a sadistic desire to create at least mischief, and preferably mental injury.

When the party broke up about midnight, she avoided being alone with Jason to say goodnight; he had to be content with a mere handshake, whereas his wife, in her capacity as a former school chum, was granted a kiss on either cheek. Even so, he managed surreptitiously to pass his card to her, on which, she was pleased to note later, she was able to find both his landline and his mobile numbers, both business and personal.

Blanche returned home the following day, but did not contact Jason that day, because she still had some research yet to do. On the Monday, however, she spent most of the day at the local reference library, where, after a long trawl through a mass of newspapers, she found the information she was looking for: the identity of Jason's current research assistant, Sukie Jameson.

That evening, Blanche decided that she should strike that very night; again she would call at dead of night, because at that time of day the human mind is more susceptible to panic. She also decided to change her speaking voice, because she had spoken to Jason a lot at Isabella's dinner party, and she did not want him to recognise her voice. Accordingly she spent most of the evening practising a range of voices, and finally settled on a husky tone, much deeper than her normal voice.

So, at about two o'clock in the morning, she called Jason on his mobile number – using her own mobile instead of her landline to make the provenance of the call more difficult to find. She hesitated for a moment before making the call, because she suddenly asked herself, 'What if his wife answers it, or his wife is there too?'

Deciding what to do in that eventuality, however, was a matter of seconds. She would tell Hermione about Jason's dirty little secrets. But if she did that, she would be unable to blackmail him. She shrugged her shoulders; it did not really matter, for her object was not principally to gain money. It was nice to have, of course, but her main reason for blackmailing was to cause pain, and if she caused pain to two people rather than one, her pleasure would be doubled. But just a minute – she knew his wife, didn't she, she had been to school with her. This reservation was also quickly rejected: she had never been especially close to Hermione, even at school, and it had been so long since she had been in contact with her that seeing her at Isabella's had been like meeting a stranger.

Blanche heard the phone ring out; as usual at that time of night, she had to wait a while for a response. At last she heard a familiar voice: 'Jason Spencer...'

Remembering just in time to use her assumed voice, Blanche replied, 'Does your wife know about Sukie Jameson?'

'Who's that speaking? Do I know you?'

'It doesn't matter. Does your wife know about Sukie Jameson?'

'What about her? She knows she's my research assistant, of course she does.'

'And does she know everything else?'

Jason remained evasive. 'Does she know what else?'

'Does she know what else you get up to with Sukie?'

'I don't get up to anything else with Sukie!'

'Oh, she's different from all the other research assistants you've had, is she?'

'I don't know what you mean.'

'Oh, come off it, Jason! Are you planning to make her sign a non-disclosure agreement like the others, or has she already signed one? And does your wife know about all the girls you've paid off in return for their silence? And does your agent Tom Bland know? And what about your constituents? Or the Chief Whip?'

'I don't know what you mean.'

'I think your constituents and the Chief Whip would like to know about them though. What say I tell them?'

'They won't believe you!'

'You're joking! It's only going to cost you a grand to stop me telling your wife, by the way. Oh, and another grand to stop me telling Tom Bland, and another grand for the Chief Whip... That makes £3000 in all...'

'I can do the maths, thank you. No, £1000 is the absolute limit!'

'£1000 will only stop me telling one of them. Which one do you want to keep it from most? Hermione? The Chief Whip? Or your agent?'

Jason made no answer, so Blanche continued, 'Or I suppose I could also tell the Chairman of your local party, or a newspaper... Which newspaper would you prefer to have your name dragged through the mud by? The *News of the World,* the *Express,* the *Sun?* It will be £1000 each to keep it out of all of them by the way...'

'The most I will pay is five grand.'

'All right. For five grand I will not say anything to your wife, your agent, to the Chief Whip or to any of the papers. Agreed?'

'Agreed.'

'And the money will be paid in cash…'

'Okay.'

'And you will leave it in an envelope bearing only your name, Jason Spencer, at the Ritz Hotel in Piccadilly. Okay?'

'Okay.'

'And don't tell the police. If I even suspect that you've been talking to the police about this, I shall go immediately to the papers. Okay?'

'Okay.'

'And you must leave it at the Ritz within 48 hours, okay?'

'Okay.'

With that, Blanche switched off her phone and terminated the call.

Two days later, Blanche called at the Ritz Hotel in Piccadilly to collect her 'winnings', as she regarded them. She went to the Reception desk, said that she had come to collect an envelope which would have been left for her, marked with the name Jason Spencer. This was a routine which she had performed several times, and which had previously been accomplished without a hitch. But on this occasion she was asked to sign a receipt, and provide her address and telephone number. She questioned this, but the answer she received from the receptionist sounded alarm bells in her head. 'Yes,' said the receptionist, 'we have a new procedure in the interests of security, because we have had occasional problems with such things as money laundering.'

Feeling she had no choice other than to comply, Blanche signed with a false name and false address, after which she left the hotel with the envelope still sealed; only when she was safely in the taxi on the way home did she check the contents, and find that the envelope did indeed contain the amount she had demanded.

When she arrived home, she paid the cab fare and went inside. Two minutes later she heard the doorbell ring, she went to the door and found herself facing two police officers.

'Would you mind telling me your name?' said one of the policemen.

Blanche thought about this for a minute, and wondered about giving the false name she had given at the Ritz, but thought better of it, because it would have been easy for the police to check the names of the residents of her apartment block.

'My name is Blanche Delaney,' she replied.

'And do you live in this flat?'

'Yes, I do.'

'How long have you been living here?'

'Oh, I don't know, several years anyway...'

'You just returned home by taxi.'

'Did I?'

'We saw you getting out of a taxi. We'd been following you home from Piccadilly. Do you deny being at the Ritz hotel earlier?'

'Did you see me there?'

'Yes, we did.'

'So there's no point in my denying it, is there?'

'Would you mind showing us the envelope you were handed at the reception desk of the hotel? We did see you accepting it, and signing for it...'

'Yes, and with a false name too,' added the other.

Blanche realised from that that she was in serious trouble, and decided to go on the attack.

'How do you know I was the person at the Ritz? I don't have any envelope to show you, so you're wasting your time!'

'I'm sorry, madam, but I'm afraid that won't wash! You see, we had a tip-off that the envelope was being picked up, and we were there when you entered the hotel. We both know that you are the person who picked up the envelope, got into a taxi, and then came here, because we followed you in the police car. So just be a good girl and show us the envelope...'

'Who gave you a tip-off about the envelope?'

'I'm not at liberty to give you that information, madam, but targeting a Member of Parliament is not the smartest thing anyone could do, especially if your accusations are false.'

'My accusations were not false! If he says they are, he's a lying toad!'

'But he's a Member of Parliament, madam!'

'But politicians lie to us all the time!'

'So why are they called Honourable Members, madam?'

'Ha! That's a good one! Jason Spencer is far from being honourable, I assure you! No woman is safe from him!'

'Do you want to make an official complaint, madam?'

'There's no point! If I did, the establishment would all close ranks! God knows how many women he's groped, just as he groped me!'

'So are you making an accusation of sexual assault, madam?'

'No, I told you there's no point.'

'So please show us the envelope you picked up from the Ritz...'

At last Blanche saw that she was facing defeat, so she went over to her bureau, opened the drawer and retrieved a foolscap envelope with the parliamentary portcullis printed on the back. The police officer opened it, and checked some of the numbers of the banknotes it contained against a list he withdrew from his pocket. 'There you are, you see, the numbers match. This list is one that the Member of Parliament we've been talking about provided us with...'

'I warned him not to tell the police!'

'Blanche Delaney,' replied the policeman, 'I am charging you with blackmailing the Member of Parliament for South Middlesex. You do not have to say anything, but anything you do say may be used in evidence against you.'

'So what happens now?' asked Blanche.

'You will accompany us to the police station, where you will be charged formally. After that, it depends on the magistrates. I advise you to call a lawyer before we go to the police station.'

But Blanche rejected the policeman's advice, bowed her head and meekly accompanied the two officers to the car.

Eventually Blanche appeared before the magistrates, although, of course, blackmail is such a serious offence that all they could do was pass it on to the Crown Court. Bail was refused, because the magistrates were not convinced that she would not repeat the behaviour, partly because of her mental state, partly because of her addiction to alcohol. Naturally, she was the subject of endless psychiatric investigations, although her defence lawyers were unable to convince the judge at her ultimate trial that she was legally insane, and therefore unfit to plead. Those investigations, coupled with the collection of a whole mass of evidence – for the charge was that she had blackmailed more than twenty people – meant that preparing for the trial was an extremely lengthy process, and it was actually more than three years after her arrest that her trial was held.

The fact that, once she had decided to become a blackmailer, she had proceeded to act in such an amateurish fashion, even after so many years, meant that the prosecution had no difficulty in proving their case; their principal concern turned out to be the immensely complex legal wrangle over whether she was fit to plead or not. In his summing-up before he passed sentence, the judge observed that at least three of her victims appeared to have been driven to commit suicide – although no charge was ever levelled at her in connection with these deaths. That, the judge went on, along with the sheer number of blackmail attempts, was sufficient to persuade him to pass the maximum sentence permitted by the law, a sentence which was eventually confirmed by the Appeal Court.

Although during the course of the case, there were innumerable allusions to the fact that one of Blanche's victims was a Member of Parliament, Jason Spencer did not give evidence to the court, nor was his name ever mentioned. A number of popular newspapers, however, did make every effort to identify the politician involved, and yet no individual's name was ever printed by any of them.

'What a vicious creature she was!' was Margaret's first comment after reading the last of David's scenarios. 'But I'm surprised she ended up in prison though, because she was obviously mentally deranged.'

'I agree with you,' said David, 'but the fact that a lot of people agree that a criminal is obviously mentally deranged, is not enough to prevent a conviction. There are very careful tests that have to be passed before someone is regarded as legally insane. I mean, I think that anybody who commits murder is obviously mentally deranged...'

'So do I,' said Margaret.

'But should that mean that none of them should be punished? That's the point really.'

'But that MP in your story went unpunished, didn't he? What a scoundrel he was, abusing all those young women...'

'I deliberately didn't put any evidence for that in my story!' said David. 'Perhaps it was a case of Blanche adding two and two and making five!'

'You authors get away with murder! You lead your readers up the garden path all the time!'

David simply laughed.

Chapter Nine

The mysterious phone call David had received at dead of night nearly a year previously, and which still persisted in giving him nightmares when he was sleeping and brain ache when he was awake, was still as much of a mystery to him as it had been on the night he had received it. And now he found himself at the beginning of his last week's work on his new book – except, of course, that once the first draft of a book is finished there is still a mountain of work to be done: editing, checking for inconsistencies, proof-reading, rewriting...

'So your book is nearly finished, is it?' asked his wife Margaret.

'If only! I still have one scenario more to write, and it's going to be the most difficult of the whole lot!'

'Why's that?'

'Because the final scenario is supposed to represent what really happened, the real explanation of the mysterious phone call that David received in the first chapter, isn't it? And if it's telling the readers what really happened, it has to be even more convincing than any that have gone before! And yet I feel as if I'm just as far away from the truth as I ever have been. God knows, I've done my best to make them all convincing...'

'Well, I think they are!'

'Bless you for that! But I want to be able to convince the sceptics too!'

'I'm sure you will...'

'I wish I had your confidence! What makes you so sure?'

'Because you have one big advantage working for you.'

'Do I? And what's that?'

'Well, just think. Imagine that you suddenly learn the truth. Would it necessarily be more believable than any of your invented stories?'

'I would like to think so!'

'Of course you would, but there's a very good chance that it might not turn out that way, isn't there?'

'Yes, okay, I suppose there is...'

'And if you did happen to stumble over the real story and it turned out to be far less convincing than any of the stories you've invented, what would you do then?'

'Well, I suppose I'd add a few details to make it more credible...'

'Could you perhaps switch the stories round, so that you present your favourite story as the one that really happened?'

'Yes, I suppose I could...'

'In that case, you're in a win-win situation!'

Why am I?'

'Well, look at it this way. You either find out the true story behind that phone call or you don't. Okay?'

'Okay.'

'And if you don't, you make one up...'

'Okay.'

'...making sure that it's more convincing than what's gone before.'

'True.'

'And if you find out the truth and then you realise that it's not really a very good story, then you either improve the story, or reject it out of hand and make one up! So you win either way!'

'Oh, I see what you mean! You mean I shouldn't let the truth get in the way of a good story!'

'Yes, if you want to put it that way...'

'But I'd still prefer to unearth the true story!'

'Of course you would, that's natural, but how likely is that? I wouldn't like to bet on it!'

'Neither would I, come to that!'

Over breakfast David deliberated, as he always did, on the direction his day's work would take, but, by the end of breakfast he was still no nearer any sort of plan for the day. He got up from the table, deposited his empty coffee cup and cereal bowl in the dishwasher, turned round, and caught sight of the telephone which stood on one of the kitchen work surfaces, and he at last found an idea coming into his head. He picked up the telephone, and dialled the number from which he had been called at dead of night nearly a year previously, a number which by now was firmly etched in his memory.

He had done this a good many times, of course, but had always heard nothing but the 'number unobtainable' tone. To his surprise, on this occasion he heard that the number was actually ringing out. This was new, he thought, but for at least half a minute nothing further occurred.

'Hello,' he suddenly heard – a woman's voice, and with a slight hint of an Irish accent, but not one he recognised. What's more, it was an older voice than the one he had heard on the only previous occasion he had been connected to that number, a voice which bore no resemblance to the one he had heard before, and which he would certainly not have been able to mistake for the voice of his own daughter.

'Hello,' he replied at last.

'Can I help you?' said the voice.

'I don't know,' David answered. 'I'm sorry, but that's not the voice I was expecting to hear...'

'Oh, I expect you were wanting to speak to my daughter, were you?'

'I don't know. Perhaps. I was just expecting a younger voice. Who's speaking?'

'This is Anna McCullough, the mother of Theresa Dulson.'

'Oh, I see,' David said, feeling he was perhaps making real progress. 'Can I speak to Theresa?'

'Not on this number you can't!'

'Does she not live there any more?'

Mrs McCullough laughed. 'In theory she does, but I don't think she'll be here in the foreseeable future.'

'Has she gone away then?'

Mrs McCullough laughed again. 'That's one way of putting it! Not that she really wanted to go where she's gone!'

David was puzzled, thinking perhaps that the lady's daughter might have recently died. 'So how long has she gone away for?'

This question was greeted with a further outbreak of laughter, but this time more prolonged. 'It depends whether she behaves herself, but even if she does, it's going to be a good few years.'

'A few years! Has she gone abroad then?'

'Oh, bless you, do you really not know?'

'No, I'm sorry, I really have no idea what you're talking about!'

'Really? Where do you live?'

'Cheltenham.'

'You live in Cheltenham, and you don't know what happened to Theresa Dulson? I can't believe it!'

'Why not?'

'Do you take the local paper?'

'The *Gloucestershire Echo*? Yes, but I don't always read it from cover to cover. Why?'

'Well, for the last few months or so, Theresa's name has been plastered all over the *Echo*!'

'Why? What has she done?'

'She's really been a naughty girl, so she has!'

'Why? What did she do?'

'I'm surprised you don't know already! Who are you?'

'My name is David Sumner, and I had a phone call from Theresa about a year ago.'

'And what do you do, Mr Sumner?'

'I'm a writer.'

'Oh, I see, you're a journalist. I'm sorry, I didn't realise you were from the press. I've said too much. Goodbye.'

And she hung up, not even giving David enough time to deny that he had anything to do with the press.

David put down the handset and walked into the lounge, where Margaret was sitting looking through the morning paper. She looked up.

'Who were you talking to?'

'I think she said her name was Anna McCullough. I just tried that number again, you know, the number that called me in the night last year...'

'And you actually got a reply this time?'

'Yes, I did. But I'm not sure that I'm any further forward! Does the name Theresa Dulson mean anything to you?'

'Should it?'

'Well, the woman I was just talking to said Theresa Dulson was her daughter, and she seemed surprised I didn't know who Theresa Dulson was, because she's apparently been all over the *Echo* recently.'

'Theresa Dulson... Yes, I thought the name rang a bell. I didn't really read all about it, but I seem to remember there was a court case at Gloucester a few months back, something to do with Cheltenham races, I think...'

'I think I'd better pop down to the library in town and have a look through past issues of the *Echo*. Do you mind if I use the car?'

'No, I don't need to go out today. Will you be back for lunch?'

'Don't know. Depends what I find out. Don't wait for me anyway – if there's something really interesting and usable, then I will probably be at the library until closing time! See you later.'

So David visited the Reference Section of Cheltenham Central Library, as he fairly often did, because, as a writer, he was constantly involved in research of one kind or another; consequently he knew a number of the staff who worked there, which was extremely useful, because there was usually someone on the staff who was able to save him a certain amount of time. And so it proved on this occasion, for, as soon as he opened the door, he spotted a man called Peter, who was especially knowledgeable about local matters.

'Peter,' he said, 'you're just the man I was hoping to see! Does the name Theresa Dulson ring any bells?'

'Good God, yes!' he exclaimed. 'She's been in and out of the *Gloucestershire Echo* for months! Haven't you been following it?'

'No, I'm afraid I missed that story! When did it start?'

'Well, if you want to start the story at the very beginning, you'd have to go back as far as last year's Cheltenham National Hunt Festival, although it wasn't until a couple of months later that the name of Theresa Dulson started to appear.'

'You mean I've got to look through a whole year's issues of the *Echo* to follow the story?'

'I'm afraid so, yes,' Peter laughed. 'But it's quietened down a bit now, now she's safely behind bars.'

'Behind bars? You mean she's been sent to prison? Her mother told me she'd been a naughty girl...'

'You know her mother?'

'Not really, but I have spoken to her. What's she been up to then?'

'You'll see for yourself when you start reading the story!'

So David started by looking at the issue of the *Gloucestershire Echo* which reported the result of the previous year's Cheltenham Gold Cup, but could see nothing relevant there apart from the name of the winner, which he already knew; although David was not especially interested in racing, for anyone who lived in Cheltenham, it was almost impossible not to be aware of the name of the Gold Cup winner.

By the time the library closed for the day, David was only about one third of the way through the pile of newspapers he had been trudging through, although, he admitted to Margaret when he finally returned home, he did already have the bones of a story which he thought matched the impact of the opening chapter. In the end he spent a whole week leafing through the *Echo*, but eventually, by the end of the following week, he had completed his version of Theresa Dulson's story, taking care, of course, to change the names of anybody involved in the real story, especially the name of Theresa herself, whom he renamed Mary Fletcher. Here is Mary's story, as written by David Sumner:

One sunny day in the middle of March, a crowd of more than 50,000 people, a large number of them Irish, had assembled in the shadow of Cleeve Hill, the highest point of the Cotswolds, to witness the running of the Cheltenham Gold Cup, the most coveted of steeplechase trophies, which has taken place every year since 1924, although the Cheltenham National Hunt Festival, of which it forms the centrepiece, was instituted in the early 1860s.

But the story which was to grip Cheltenham – and, indeed the whole of both the British and Irish racing fraternity for most of the following year – had nothing to do with the Gold Cup itself, but with one of the minor races; the Gold Cup is always run in the middle of the afternoon, and is generally preceded and followed by three other races, all over hurdles or enormous fences. In terms of the Cheltenham National Hunt Festival, of course, *minor* is a relative term, for the quality of the horses, the amount of the prize money to be won, and the size of the crowd all combine to transform even the least important of the races on the card into an event which would be considered major at any lesser venue than Prestbury Park.

The race in question was the penultimate race on the card, a steeplechase handicap on the Old Course, as it was known, whose entries were limited to four year olds. By now some of the enormous crowd had already left, but even so, the 'Cheltenham Roar', which greets the start of every race, was hardly diminished in volume when the race began.

The difference in atmosphere, however, was more noticeable at the end of the race, for, whereas the noise at the end of the Gold Cup nearly matches the volume of the famous 'Roar', especially this particular year, when the Gold Cup had been won by the favourite, on the occasion of this minor race the only people cheering were the few who had backed the winning outsider, supported enthusiastically by most of the bookmakers, who considered a 100-1 winner as giving them an opportunity to recoup some of the losses they had suffered in the big race of the day.

The result of the race did not seem out of the ordinary at the time, for, even at the Cheltenham

Festival, 100-1 winners are not unknown – the Gold Cup itself famously had a 100-1 winner, *Norton's Coin*, in 1981 – but once the bookmakers had done their sums afterwards, stories started to circulate in racing circles about the losses that many of them had had to bear; there had been, it seemed, very few bookmakers who had not been obliged to pay out on a £1,000 stake, which means that the bookmaker has to pay out £100,000, plus, of course, returning the original stake. At first the stories were regarded as merely racing gossip, but, by the end of April, such august publications as the *Racing Post* were taking the stories much more seriously, even going so far as to report that the police were beginning to take an active interest.

The principal reason for the *Racing Post* to give credence to what they had originally regarded as 'gossip' was the track history of the horse on which the bookmakers had reportedly lost so much money. *Your Family* was a four-year-old, which, prior to its successful appearance at Cheltenham, had only raced at less prestigious courses such as Market Rasen, Hereford, Southwell and Lichfield, although it had had one outing, a month prior to the Cheltenham Festival, at Chepstow, the venue of the Welsh Grand National, where it had seemingly confirmed its potential by coming next to last in a field of seven; and yet here it was just one month later, winning at Cheltenham by several lengths, and with the owner pocketing £50,000 prize money!

The first time the police admitted that they were taking an interest in the outcome of the race was when they announced that a Cheltenham woman named Mary Fletcher was helping them with their inquiries two or three months after the race in question; at the same time there were reports of police visits having been made to a yard where *Your Family* had been stabled for the duration of his visit to Cheltenham, and to the residence of the horse's owner in Staffordshire. Reports also said that two trainers' yards in Ireland had been visited by the Irish police, although there was so far no confirmation that this had any connection to *Your Family*'s win.

Mary Fletcher was a divorcee living in Bishop's Cleeve, a village on the northern outskirts of Cheltenham, just on the other side of the racecourse from the town itself. She was in her late twenties, and worked as a cleaner at a factory making electronic components for the aircraft industry; since her divorce, she had been living alone. Her ex-husband was now in prison, having been convicted of assaulting Mary repeatedly ever since their marriage, which had lasted only five or six years, the last straw having been when her husband arrived home drunk one evening and she had had the temerity to say she wanted a divorce. Her immediate reward was a black eye, followed by a stab wound in the arm a few hours later; that the outcome of the knife attack was not even more serious was because she had heard him come into the bedroom and parried the blow with a pillow, screaming so loud that her next-door neighbours, who occupied the other half of her semi, started banging on the wall, whereupon her husband fled and she was able to summon the police. Never had she felt so relieved that the walls separating her house from the neighbour's were so thin. As a result of the attack her husband was charged with Grievous Bodily Harm, found guilty, and sentenced to five years' imprisonment.

One evening, Mary had been in her local pub with a few friends, when Mavis, a particular friend with whom she worked, had asked her if she would like to make 'a few bob' simply by making a phone call in the middle of the night. She had been reluctant to begin with, but, after Mavis had assured her that the risk to her was low because she would not even be aware of what the operation was meant to achieve, nor even the identity of the person she would be telephoning, or the person who was running the operation, she acquiesced, and was especially pleased when she discovered that her 'few bob' would actually amount to £500!

At first, because of Mavis's assurances that there was no risk involved unless she asked too many questions and was given a lot of information which she did not really need to know, Mary did not inquire too closely. 'You will receive instructions who to call and when, and the exact words to use,' she had said, 'you will not be told the person's name or where they live, and the message you pass on will not mean anything to you.'

But Mary was by nature an inquisitive person, and soon she wanted to know more. 'When will I get the money?' she asked her friend. 'Will I get paid in advance?'

'No, I'm afraid not,' came the reply. 'It will depend on whether everything works out.'

'So how long will I have to wait?'

'Not too long. Probably two or three days, I should think.'

'And when will I have to make the phone call?'

'I don't know. Not for a few more weeks anyway.'

'How will I know who to ring?'

'You'll receive written instructions.'

'Who from?'

'I don't know.'

'Will the instructions come through the post?'

'No, they will be pushed through your letter box.'

'It's not something dodgy, is it?'

'It's not something you need to worry about, as long as everything goes to plan. And the less you know, the less you have to worry about.'

'Okay,' Mary replied, 'but when is this all going to happen?'

'About the middle of March, I think.'

'Oh, I hope it doesn't clash with the Cheltenham Festival! I've got a couple of Irish chaps coming to stay for the races...'

'Have you? asked Mavis anxiously. 'In that case, I think I'd better tell my friend that you don't want to be involved.'

'But I do want to be involved!' Mary insisted. 'I could really do with that 500 quid!'

'Tell me about the Irishmen. Are they paying you?'

'Oh yes, of course they are!'

'Have they been to stay with you before?'

'Yes, they've been coming for two or three years.'

'Oh, in that case I should think it will be all right. Just don't tell them about the phone call you have to make, that's all.'

'I won't see much of them, I don't suppose. They always go out drinking every evening after the races, and they're not really interested in anything I do anyway. All they ever talk about is horses and racing...'

'Well, just keep your mouth shut while they're there!'

'Is the phone call something to do with the races then?'

'I don't know. I've probably told you too much already. Don't ask me any more questions about it!'

Mary obediently stopped asking questions, although there were many more that she would have liked to ask, for she was feeling increasingly anxious about what she had become involved in.

She did not hear any more about it until the day before the race meeting started, when her two Irish visitors turned up on her doorstep. She opened the door and greeted them. 'Oh look,' said one of them, bending down to pick up an envelope which was lying on the doormat, 'you've got some mail.' He handed the letter to Mary, who glanced at it and put it in her pinafore pocket without further comment.

'I'll show you your room,' Mary said.

'No, there's no need, we know where everything is, and we're going straight out anyway. We probably won't see you again till breakfast time!'

'I know you two by now!' she joked. 'Just don't wake me up when you do come home!'

'Don't worry! We know the rules of the house by now. We'll be quiet as church mice!'

Ten minutes later she heard them go out again, whereupon she went into the kitchen, sat down, and retrieved the letter from her pinafore pocket. She opened the envelope and found a single sheet of paper, on which there was a typewritten message. At the top of the sheet she saw a telephone number in large type, which, because of its 01242 area code, she immediately recognised as a Cheltenham number. Below the number appeared the following message:

1. Call the above number between 02.00 and 02.30 on 13 March. The person you are calling will be expecting your call. DO NOT GIVE YOUR NAME.

2. Ask the following question: 'Are you listening?' If you do not ask this question, the person you are calling will hang up.

3. When the person you are calling confirms that he/she is listening, give the following message: 'This is very important. I did not call the police. It was your family who called the police.' IT IS VERY IMPORTANT THAT YOU USE THESE EXACT WORDS.

4. Hang up. Do not enter into conversation with the person you are calling.

5. Destroy this paper and do not discuss its contents with anyone.

She read the letter twice, then put it away in a safe place until shortly before she was due to make the call, which would be the following night.

On the night in question she retrieved the letter from its hiding place and, having checked to make sure that her temporary lodgers were not in the house, she rehearsed the delivery of the message. By midnight her visitors had still not come home, nor at one o'clock either; that was not especially strange, because they would normally come home by taxi, and in the three or four hours after midnight in Cheltenham race week, those seeking a taxi were always far in excess of the taxis available. On a number of previous occasions, they had had to walk all the way from the centre of Cheltenham to Bishop's Cleeve, a distance of three or four miles.

But the nearer the hands of the clock approached the time at which she was due to make her call, the more nervous she felt. At about a quarter to two she heard the front door open, and then two pairs of feet made their way up the stairs. She held her breath until she was sure the visitors were safely upstairs, then took out the letter again. Next she heard a door open and close, and, after that, the sound of a toilet being flushed, and she waited until she heard the same sequence of sounds one more time before she was satisfied that the two men were now safely in their bedrooms and that she would not be disturbed.

She looked at the clock: it was now ten past two. Her pulse was racing, her heart was thumping, and she felt herself breaking out into a cold sweat. But she could not afford to postpone the call a moment longer, she decided, or she would risk forfeiting the £500 on which she was counting so much. She picked up the phone, and prepared to dial the number.

Just as she began dialling, she heard the sound of a door opening, and then footsteps on the upstairs landing. She waited a second until all was quiet again, then, heart still thumping, she dialled the number.

'Are you listening?' she said as soon as someone responded, but she heard no reply to her question. She asked the question again, and then a third time, before she received the assurance she required. But her instructions had said that the person she was calling would be expecting her call; surely, she thought, if this man was expecting a call, she would not have had to ask three times if he were listening? Never mind, she told herself, that's not my problem, I just need to deliver the message. So she continued: 'This is very important. I did not call the police. It was your family who called the police.'

'What? What are you talking about? What do you mean? I don't know what you're talking about...'

She came very near to answering his question, or making a comment upon his apparent lack of readiness, but then remembered her instruction not to engage in conversation, and hung up.

Then she began to worry about what she had done. The man she had been talking to had evidently not expected her call. How could that be? Perhaps she had misdialled. After all, she recollected, she had been in quite a state when she made the call, partly because of her fear of being overheard by the Irish lodgers, partly because, despite the assurances that Mavis had given her, she was already worried about becoming involved with some kind of shady deal.

She sat down at the kitchen table and thought about the situation, of which two aspects caused her particular anxiety. If somehow she had called the wrong person – even accidentally – did that mean she would forfeit the £500 she was expecting? And, if she had been speaking to the wrong person, what might that man do? What if he were to call her back, what would she say? The more she thought about it, the more anxious she became, because another scenario came into her mind: what if the organiser of the operation which Mavis had persuaded her to join were to call and ask her why she had not made the call, what would she say to him? And, given that her pay-out was to be £500 for doing very little, the operation, whatever it was, must have been worth a good deal more; so what fate might await her if she had unwittingly caused the operation to fail? Should she perhaps pretend that the phone had been out of order, and so she had been unable to make the call as planned? But that could only provide a plausible answer if the phone really were out of order...

Seized by panic, she found a little screwdriver which was always kept in one of the kitchen drawers in case of minor electrical faults, then unscrewed the top of the telephone junction box which was also located in the kitchen, and proceeded to disconnect one of the wires inside, before replacing the junction box's cover. Having done that, she lifted the handset of the telephone to verify that the line was dead: it was, so she finally went to bed.

Not that she slept, of course, for she was far too agitated to be able to sleep the sleep of the just. Nor could she afford to have a lie-in, even if, being a cleaner, she did not need to go into the factory until the workers went home at the end of their day, because she needed to cook breakfast for her race-going visitors, who relied on a substantial breakfast 'to see them through the day', as they always said. Moreover, when the visitors came down for breakfast she needed to respond amicably to their habitual banter. At last she had the house to herself again, and went back to bed; this time she slept until mid-afternoon. At about six o'clock in the evening the two visitors returned home, and in remarkably good spirits.

'Mary!' one of them said, 'We've had a fantastic day, and it's all thanks to you, so before we go out and spend all our winnings, we'd like to give you this.' So saying, he presented her with a £50 note.

'What's this in aid of?' she exclaimed.

'Well,' one of them replied, 'it's all because I went to the loo last night, and I heard you talking to somebody on the phone. I didn't listen, honest I didn't, but I did hear you say the words 'your family'. And then when I was looking through the race card this morning I spotted that there was one of the runners whose name was *Your Family*. Well, it was too much of a coincidence to ignore, so I backed it.'

'Truly scientific his betting system is, to be sure!' his mate commented.

'Well, at least it won!' his friend countered. 'And at 100-1 too! So I won £1000! Anyway, we're going out on the town now. Don't bother to wait up for us!'

Within five minutes Mary was on her own again, and, although she was happy with her unexpected gift, the fact that one of them had overheard her phone conversation rekindled her anxiety, a degree of uneasiness which redoubled when it occurred to her eventually that the phone call she was supposed to have made was part of a big racing scam!

If Mary had been aware of the true extent of the operation into which she had been recruited, she would have been even more worried than she was, for, as she had surmised, a pay-out of £500 for making a simple phone call implied a seriously massive operation, which had been over a year in the planning, and which involved at least two trainers, one in England, one in Ireland, two owners, one jockey, one vet, and numerous little people like Mary, who did not know enough about the operation to suspect that it was shady.

The success of the scam depended upon nobody suspecting that *Your Family* was not all he seemed, for the horse who had won the race in question was a totally different horse, from a totally different yard. The replacement horse, the 'ringer', was actually a year older than *Your Family*, and would have been ineligible anyway because he was no longer a four year old. But even if he had been eligible, he would have been carrying much more weight if he had been entered legitimately, for older horses are regarded by handicappers as being more experienced. What's more, the ringer had already won two or three races in Ireland under the name of *Clontarf Belle*; to a layman it would have been difficult to distinguish one from the other, but, thanks to the paperwork signed by a crooked vet, he was able to deceive even the professionals. In addition, *Clontarf Belle* was able to benefit from *Your Family*'s abysmal track record because *Your Family*'s failure to perform creditably in any of the races in which he had previously taken part would in itself have given him a considerable advantage over the rest of the field, but, coupled with the experience of *Clontarf Belle*, the outcome was a foregone conclusion. Fortunately for the perpetrators of the scam, the fact that a price of 100-1 is not especially unusual in National Hunt racing, even at Cheltenham, particularly in the minor races, was not sufficient for the result to have been regarded immediately with suspicion.

However, there was some concern expressed by a number of bookmakers, especially the small-time bookmakers. It began with one or two chatting among themselves about colleagues who had been in deep difficulties or who had actually gone out of business, for a loss of £100,000 would be very difficult for a small-time bookmaker to take. Eventually the police began to take an interest, initially because of the chatter, but when they eventually started to collate their findings, they discovered that some of the big betting firms had also taken several bets of £1,000, so there were very few indeed who had emerged unscathed. As the total sum of client winnings was well in excess of £1 million, with only the biggest firms having taken more than one such bet, a decision was taken by the police that further investigation was required, for such facts as were known implied something much more than coincidence. But the plan had been put together so skilfully, and executed so discreetly, that the police needed a slice of luck of the magnitude of that enjoyed by Mary's Irish lodgers, so it was some time before their investigative efforts bore any fruit, and, extraordinarily, the breakthrough they were seeking came from Mary herself.

Two or three weeks after the race meeting, Mary had still not received her £500, so one evening, she went to the same pub where she had made the original agreement with Mavis, and confronted her as soon as she saw her.

'When am I going to get my money?' she demanded.

'What money?'

'The money I earned by making that phone call.'

'What phone call?'

'The phone call you asked me to make.'

'I don't remember asking you to make a phone call.'

'You did!' Mary insisted. 'You said that all I needed to do was make a simple phone call, and I would be paid £500!'

'I never did!'

Mary was incandescent, for Mavis persisted in denying her involvement. But Mary continued repeating that Mavis had asked her to make a phone call; moreover, with each repetition, she gave more details of the instructions she had been given and was now speaking so loudly that Mavis began to feel alarmed. At length she felt so desperate that she said to Mary, 'But you didn't make the bloody phone call, did you?'

'How do you know I didn't?'

'Because the person you were supposed to be calling said he never received the call, and that's why you aren't getting paid!'

'I thought you said you didn't remember asking me to make a phone call! So how come you know that I didn't make the call, tell me that, you scum bag!'

Mary was nonplussed, and reverted to her original profession of ignorance: 'I haven't the first idea what you're talking about!'

'You'll find out soon enough!' shouted Mary, as she stormed out of the pub.

Half an hour later, Mavis was feeling so despondent that she decided to call it a night and go home, so she left the pub and went out into the car park. Just as she was opening the door of her car to get in and drive home, Mary suddenly appeared out of the shadows: she had been lying in wait for Mavis to emerge.

'I'll get you, you bitch!' Mary screamed.

'Get away from me!' Mavis yelled in return, taking a swing with her handbag towards Mary's head.

Immediately Mary retaliated, wielding a knife with which she stabbed Mavis in the shoulder, whereupon Mavis screamed so loudly that a number of people ran out of the pub to find out what was going on in the car park. A couple of men gave Mavis first aid, while two or three more restrained Mary, until finally an ambulance came to take Mavis to the hospital; ultimately the police arrived to take Mary into custody.

Mary appeared at Cheltenham Magistrate's Court the following day, where she was remanded in custody. Two or three months later she appeared at Gloucester County Court, on a charge of attempted murder: the jury found her not guilty of that charge, but guilty of occasioning Grievous Bodily Harm, and she was sent to prison for five years.

It was some time before the police finally unravelled the details of the betting coup, but unravel it they did. As part of their investigation of Mary, they searched her house, and found the letter giving her the instructions to make the late night phone call; she had been in such a panic that she had forgotten to destroy it as she had been instructed.

The following year two racehorse trainers, a jockey, a vet, and several businessmen were convicted of conspiring to commit fraud, and were each sent to prison for an even longer period than was Mary. As for Mary's two Irish guests, nobody came to take their winnings away, and the following year they were completely mystified at getting no answer when they tried to telephone Mary to see if they could stay with her during race week again!

'Well, I never!' exclaimed David's wife once she had finished reading David's final story. 'That's a cracking story, darling! Well done! I never expected it to turn out like that! I was expecting to read the name Theresa Dulson. What happened to her?'

'Oh, I changed her name, just to be on the safe side! For Theresa Dulson, read Mary Fletcher.'

'Oh, I see. And did all that really happen?'

More or less,' replied David. 'I put in one or two details when I found there was a gap in what I'd been able to find out, but I reckoned I was free to do that, given what you said to me...'

'Remind me what I said to you,' said Margaret. 'I've forgotten...'

'You said the author is God...'

THE END

The Author

Although he will shortly turn 87 years of age, Tony Whelpton is still working.

He has been writing books for forty years, but turned to fiction late in life, and has been so successful that he wishes he had started earlier! He is the author of thirty or so school and college text books – mostly in French – as well as two books on cricket, and a history of the Cheltenham Bach Choir, of which he became Vice-President after retiring from singing at the age of 80.

He was born in Nottingham, England, in January 1933, and was educated at High Pavement Grammar School (where he was taught English by the 1974 Booker Prize winner Stanley Middleton), and at the Universities of London and Lille.

He taught French for many years, first in secondary schools, then at university level. He is also an experienced journalist and broadcaster, and, for more than a quarter of a century, was universally recognised as one of the most influential authorities in the British school examination system.

His first novel, *Before the Swallow Dares,* was published in 2012, when Tony was 79. This was shortly followed by another, *The Heat of the Kitchen,* then another, the popular *Billy's War*. A sequel to *Billy's War, There's No Pride in Prejudice,* was published in 2016.

Since then Tony has continued to publish a novel a year, and shows no sign of stopping yet! An important milestone for Tony was reached in 2017, when the prestigious *Times and Sunday Times Cheltenham Literature Festival* chose to invite him to talk about and read from his novel *A Change of Mind*, which had just been published. Two more novels followed: *High Time* was published in 2018, followed by *At Dead of Night* in 2019.

Seven novels in seven years is not bad going for any author, but is quite remarkable for one who is as advanced in years as Tony. His health remains pretty good, with only minor problems (it is typical of Tony that he regards two hip replacements, one knee replacement and an operation on his spine as 'minor problems').

Tony's attitude to life is that it is there for living and, in particular, getting old is not an excuse for sitting around doing nothing; one of his favourite quotations comes from the French cellist Paul Tortelier: 'Everybody should die young – but as late in life as possible'. Now you understand why Tony is still writing!

If you would like to know more about Tony and about his work, check out his website at www.literarylounge.co.uk and follow him on Twitter (@TonyWhelpton1) or like his Facebook page Tony Whelpton Novelist.

Even more importantly, if you have enjoyed reading this book, please take a few minutes to write a review on the Amazon website!

Lightning Source UK Ltd.
Milton Keynes UK
UKHW010858110819
347745UK00001B/23/P

9 781916 000018